"I'm better off staying single, Martin," Julia said.

Martin almost gasped out loud but caught himself in time. Julia not ever marry? He could hardly contemplate such a situation.

"Why do you say that?" he asked.

She shrugged. "Love hurts too much. If I don't fall in love, I can't be hurt. It's that simple. I get to say what happens in my life and I'm not at the whim and pleasure of someone who doesn't really care about me."

He nodded his assent. "It is true that if you don't love, you won't be hurt. But you also won't have the joy. And besides, if you marry a man who really loves you, he would never want to hurt you."

Julia was quiet for a moment, her face filled with such sadness that he thought she might cry. "I have loved before but he didn't love me in return. He abandoned me when I needed him most. It hurt more than I can say. Love isn't all it's cracked up to be, Martin. It can be brutal, cruel and destructive."

He realized what she said was true. And yet, he couldn't give up hope.

Not for her. And not for himself…

Leigh Bale is a *Publishers Weekly* bestselling author. She is the winner of the prestigious Golden Heart® Award and is a finalist for the Gayle Wilson Award of Excellence and the Booksellers' Best Award. The daughter of a retired US forest ranger, she holds a BA in history. Married in 1981 to the love of her life, Leigh and her professor husband have two children and two grandkids. You can reach her at leighbale.com.

Books by Leigh Bale

Love Inspired

Colorado Amish Courtships

Runaway Amish Bride
His Amish Choice
Her Amish Christmas Choice

Men of Wildfire

Her Firefighter Hero
Wildfire Sweethearts
Reunited by a Secret Child

The Road to Forgiveness
The Forest Ranger's Promise
The Forest Ranger's Husband
The Forest Ranger's Child
Falling for the Forest Ranger
Healing the Forest Ranger
The Forest Ranger's Return

Visit the Author Profile page at Harlequin.com for more titles.

Her Amish Christmas Choice

Leigh Bale

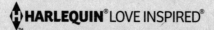

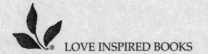

LOVE INSPIRED BOOKS

ISBN-13: 978-1-335-47950-1

Her Amish Christmas Choice

www.Harlequin.com

Printed in U.S.A.

I returned, and saw under the sun,
that the race is not to the swift,
nor the battle to the strong, neither yet
bread to the wise, nor yet riches to men of
understanding, nor yet favour to men of skill;
but time and chance happeneth to them all.
—*Ecclesiastes* 9:11

To my very own Rose, who has brought me more joy than I ever thought possible.

Chapter One

"*Hallo?*"

Julia Rose jerked, startled. The two nails she'd been holding between her pursed lips dropped to the wooden planks of the front porch and bounced off into the weedy flower bed.

She swiveled around on the rickety ladder and caught a glimpse of a tall man standing directly behind her. She didn't have time to return his greeting. The leather gloves she wore were overly large and caused her to lose her grasp on the heavy hammer. It followed the nails, thudding to the wooden porch below. The ladder wobbled and she fought to retain her grip on the tall post she'd been holding upright with her left hand. For fifteen minutes, she'd struggled to get it in just the right spot so she could nail it into place. Now, it slid sideways. Without its support, the heavy canopy above sagged dangerously near her head. The overly stressed timbers gave a low groan and she widened her eyes.

"*Acht gewwe!*" the man called in a foreign language.

A sickening crack sounded above and Julia scrambled down the ladder. Like a zipper coming undone, the nails holding the awning to the side of the building pinged into the air as the canopy tore away from the outer wall and knocked her to the ground. She gasped in pain as the ruined wood continued its descent toward her.

With a cry of alarm, she curled against the side of the wall, protecting her head with her arms. She was vaguely aware of the man shielding her, taking the brunt of the weight against his own back.

"Oof!"

She glanced up and found his face no more than a breath away. She gazed into his eyes, catching the subtle scent of licorice. His muscular arms held her tight as another piece of the canopy bludgeoned him with a shocking thump. He jerked at the impact but made no sound. For several seconds, they both held perfectly still. She felt uncomfortable with his close proximity but couldn't move away just then.

"Alles fit? Are you all right?" His voice sounded low and calm, like the approach of thunder off in the distance.

"I think so." She stared in fascination, captivated by his piercing blue eyes… The kind of eyes that could see deep inside a person's heart and know exactly what they were thinking. In those brief moments, she took in his plain clothes, his angular face, short auburn hair and a faint smattering of freckles across the bridge of his nose. No doubt he spent hours working outside in the sun.

"Mar-tin! Mar-tin, are you okay?"

Julia looked up and saw a boy of approximately fifteen years standing in front of the ruined porch. Dressed identical to the man, his short, stocky build was accented by plain black pants, a blue chambray shirt, black suspenders and a black felt hat.

They were Amish!

"*Ja*, I'm okay, Hank." The man holding onto Julia let her go and moved back with a slight grimace.

She scurried to safety, standing beyond the reach of the broken canopy. With her out of the way, the man jerked to the side and let the remaining boards sag to the ground. They hung there like a great, broken beast.

"It'll be all right now. You'll be okay." The boy named Hank patted Julia's arm, looking directly into her eyes as he earnestly searched her expression for distress.

Hank was a stranger and again she felt uncomfortable by the invasion of her personal space but saw no guile in his dark eyes. He looked genuinely concerned for her welfare. His brown eyes slanted upward and he had an open, childlike expression. As she took in his reddish-blond hair and small, flat nose, she recognized instantly that Hank must have Down Syndrome.

"Y-yes. I'm fine," she said.

He smiled wide, pushing his wire-rimmed spectacles up the bridge of his nose. He looked so innocent and sincere that she had to return his infectious smile.

"Mar-tin, she's okay. How about you? Are you okay?" Hank asked, his accent heavy.

"*Ja*, I'm all right," the man named Martin said.

But Julia had her doubts. He stood slowly and side-stepped the rubble, stumbling before he regained his footing. As he rubbed his left arm, a flash of pain crossed his face. He clenched his eyes closed for a brief moment but didn't utter a single word of complaint. His black felt hat had been knocked from his head. He opened his eyes and glanced at her, a look of worry creasing his handsome forehead.

"You are not injured?" he asked, his voice tinged with an edge of authority.

She shook her head. "No, thanks to you."

She coughed and waved a hand at the dust filling the air. Martin had used his own body to shield her from the heavy boards. She considered what might have happened if he hadn't been there.

He stood up straight, his great height a sharp contrast to Hank's. "You should rope off this area so no one walks by unaware and puts themselves in danger."

"Yes, I'll do that. Th-thank you," she said, still breathless and amazed by the ordeal.

"You're *willkomm*." He brushed the dust off his clothes.

"Mar-tin, I saw what happened and came to help." Hank's face was lit by an eager expression.

"*Ach*, you sure did. I'm glad you were here." Martin rested a hand on Hank's shoulder and the boy smiled at the man with adoration. The two looked alike, yet Martin didn't seem old enough to be Hank's father. Perhaps they were brothers?

"Thank the *gut* Lord no one was seriously injured today." Martin flexed his right arm as if testing it for soundness. He arched his waist, his blue chambray shirt stretching taut across his solid chest.

Hmm, very odd. Though she understood his comment, she realized he was mixing English with some other language.

He looped his thumbs through his black suspenders. The tips of his heavy work boots were almost covered by the hem of his plain gray pants. A brisk October wind ruffled his short hair, but he didn't seem to feel the chill. Within two weeks, it would be November. Julia pulled her own jacket tighter in front of her, ever conscious that winter was fast approaching.

When the man reached to scoop up his hat and placed it on his head, she tried to look away. Since she'd never seen an Amish man before—even when she'd lived in Kansas, where she knew a few settlements existed—she couldn't help staring. When she and her mom had recently moved here to Riverton, Colorado, she hadn't expected to find any Amish. But more than that, she wondered what he was doing here at her place.

"Who are you?" she asked, trying not to sound rude.

He bent over and tossed the heavy post aside, his movements strong and athletic. "I am Martin Hostetler and this is my younger brother Hank. Carl Nelson, the attorney in town, told me you are looking for a handyman to fix up your place. I've done work for Carl in the past. If the owner of your business is available, I'd like to speak with him about a job."

Him. He thought the owner of the store was a man.

A stab of pain pierced Julia's heart. Her father had never owned this rundown hovel; he'd died just eleven months earlier after a valiant battle with pancreatic cancer. Both Julia and her mother missed him more than they could say.

"I'm the owner, Julia Rose," she said, lifting her chin higher and trying to force a note of confidence into her voice.

After her father became sick, she'd supported her parents off the proceeds of her handmade soap. Mom had lupus and couldn't help much. As an only child, Julia had stepped in to care for them. It had been a meager living but Julia was grateful her mother had taught her the craft. She'd learned to make lotions, creams, facial masks and lip balms, too. But if they didn't get the soap store up and running within the next six weeks, she wouldn't have time to make more soap, which could jeopardize her wholesale contract.

"*Ach*, you are the owner? But I thought Walter Rose still owned this building." Martin blinked, gazing at the drab brown structure with surprise.

"That's right. He was my grandfather. But he died a couple of months ago and left everything to me."

"*Ach*, I didn't know. Mr. Nelson didn't tell me that. My condolences."

"*Ja*, my condenses, too," Hank said, struggling to pronounce the word with his thick tongue.

Julia couldn't hold back a small laugh, to which the boy smiled. It was a blunt, open smile that sparkled his dark eyes and lit up his face with joy.

She glanced at Martin, seeing the genuine compassion in his eyes. She also felt sad for her grandfather's passing but couldn't really miss him. Not when she'd never met the man. Now that she was twenty-three, she mourned the fact that she'd never gotten to know her grandpa. As an only child, she had lived a rather lonely life and longed for family and friends. She thought she'd found that when she became engaged to Dallin almost two years earlier. But it didn't last. And all she knew about her grandfather was that he had not gotten along well with her father. At all. The two had a falling-out years before her birth and hadn't spoken since. She had no idea why.

"Mr. Nelson sent you here?" she asked.

"*Ja*, he said you need a handyman to help with repairs."

Carl Nelson was the only attorney in town and had

contacted Julia after Grandpa Walt died. Located at the end of Main Street, the store was rundown but spacious, with lots of potential for growth. Her grandfather had lived in the two-bedroom apartment upstairs, which included a small bathroom and kitchen-living area. But they had no electricity in spite of having turned the power back on. Julia wasn't sure, but she thought there was a problem with the fuse box. Apparently, the same situation had existed while Grandpa Walt had lived here. She and her mother had arrived in town two weeks earlier and were still using the gas and kerosene lamps he'd left behind.

"I definitely need a handyman," Julia said as she explained the situation to Martin. "With my father being sick and not enough money to pay the bills, we had to shut off the power back home in Kansas. I've contacted an electrician here in Riverton, but it'll cost a lot to replace the fuse panel and upgrade the system. We need to wait until I have more funds. But it's no matter. We kind of got used to doing without electricity. We live a simple life."

He nodded. "You are better off without it and I don't need it for my work."

"That's good. Paying you is my priority right now, so I can get my studio and store up and running. Do you know carpentry work?" she asked, wondering how he could do the job without a power drill and electric saw.

Another nod, a slight smile curving his lips. "*Ja*, and plumbing, but I don't use electricity."

Though she'd never met an Amish person, she'd heard the use of electricity was against their religious values, or something like that.

"But there's just one thing you need to know... Hank

works with me. I promise he won't be a bother or slow me down. Is that okay?" Martin asked.

As he listened to this exchange, Hank's eyes widened, his mouth hanging slack. His expression looked so intense that she didn't have the heart to say no.

"Of course. That will be fine," she said, realizing she had no one else to hire. Not in a town this size. Thankfully, the money Grandpa Walt had left her would allow her to pay a handyman.

Hank's eyes sparkled with pure delight. "*Ach*, I work hard, too. I help a lot."

She returned his smile, a feeling of deep compassion filling her heart. She liked this boy and his brother. All her life, she'd wished she had a brother or sister of her own. Someone to help look after her ailing parents. Since her breakup with her lying ex-fiancé, she'd felt so alone and it warmed her heart to see how kind these two brothers were to each other.

"*Gut.* What needs to be done?" Martin asked.

Julia shrugged, brushing at her faded blue jeans. "As you can see, the front porch is falling apart, there are two gaping holes in one of the walls of my workroom, and I need to install counters, cabinets and shelving in the area where I plan to make and sell my soap."

Martin nodded, seeming to mentally calculate how to accomplish these tasks. "You make soap?"

"Yes, among other things. I sell my products nationwide. But since the soap needs to cure for four or five weeks, I'm eager to get some made before my next contract comes due the first of February. I supply handmade soaps to KostSmart."

He looked at her without recognition. Obviously, this Amish man didn't get out much if he'd never heard of the giant supermarket chain. But since they didn't have a KostSmart here in Riverton, she figured it was unimportant. As long as the town had a postal service, she could ship her goods anywhere in the world.

"Follow me." Julia slipped through the front door. "The porch is the first thing I need repaired, so we can walk inside without fearing for our lives."

"*Ja*, I see that." Martin showed a wry smile as he trailed after her. Upon entering the spacious room, he pulled the hat off his head. Hank did likewise, copying his brother's every movement.

Wow! They sure were polite. Dallin, her ex-fiancé, had never treated her so courteously. Never said *please* or *thank you*. Never asked how she was. How it hurt to discover he was coming over not to spend time with her, but to be near her former best friend, Debbie. But Dallin had loved kids. Julia had longed for a family of her own and thought she would have it with him. Losing her fiancé and best friend all at once had broken her heart and left her feeling more alone than ever before.

She mentally shook her head. No! She was not going to think about Dallin. She'd already cried buckets of tears over him. She and Mom had a fresh start and it didn't include her two-timing fiancé and ex–best friend. But he'd taught her one important lesson: never trust a man.

"Exactly how skilled a carpenter and plumber are you?" she asked.

"I am skilled enough for the work you need done." Martin's voice was filled with confidence and a sweeping honesty. But Dallin's lies had taught her to question everything.

"Can you expand on your experience, please?" she asked.

"*Ja...*" Martin took a deep breath. "I have helped the men in my *Gmay* build seven barns, nine houses, a variety of sheds and outbuildings and many pieces of furniture in my father's home."

"What is a *Gmay*?" she asked.

"The Amish community here in Riverton. Members of our congregation follow the same *Ordnung* and attend church together. We also rely on one another in all facets of everyday life," he said.

"*Ordnung?*" she asked, enthralled by his use of new words and curious to know their meaning.

"The unwritten rules that govern our community."

"Oh. Then, I suppose you are skilled enough," she said.

Still, a lance of skepticism speared her. Although the building she owned was quite shabby, Julia had a vision of a happy place to live. Some nails and paint could transform this store beautifully. She was determined to make it work. Determined to secure a future for her and Mom. She must! She was alone now and had promised her father before his death that she'd look after her mother. After all, Mom was the only family she had left.

Martin glanced around the enormous room filled with boxes, broken furniture and piles of junk.

"Except for the old woodstove, I'd like everything hauled off to the dump," she said.

"*Ja*, I can do that. Hank will help me," Martin said.

Hank nodded eagerly. Julia didn't see how they could carry everything off without a truck, but she didn't say so. She had already cleared tons of debris from their living quarters upstairs and stacked it neatly in the backyard until they could haul it off. When she considered the bit of money Grandpa Walt had left her, she didn't want to spend it on a car. Although she had a driver's license, they'd sold their broken-down truck to pay bills many months ago. When she and Mom had moved to Colorado, they'd shipped their few possessions here, then traveled to town via bus. The general store, post office and bank were within walking distance, so they shouldn't need a vehicle.

"What do you charge?" She braced herself, but there was no need. Martin requested such a low hourly rate for himself and Hank that she was compelled to offer more.

Martin shook his head. "*Ne*, the price I have asked is sufficient for our needs."

"But...but I don't want to cheat you," she said.

"You won't. I trust you. It is a fair price for both of us," he insisted, his gaze never wavering.

Hank didn't say a word, just gawked at his brother with complete confidence.

"All right. When can you start?" she asked, hoping he didn't let her down.

"Right now. But we don't work on Sundays. I'll get my tools."

He headed outside with Hank. She watched them through the grimy windows that desperately needed cleaning. While many people worked or played on Sunday, she figured Martin and his family must go to church. With her father's death and mother's illness, she'd been thinking about God quite a bit lately. She'd been hungering to know and understand His place in her life. She'd even considered going to church, to see if she could learn more about Him, though she hadn't had time to act on that goal yet.

It was then she noticed a horse and buggy-wagon, tied beneath the tall elm tree that edged the five-space parking lot in front of the store. Martin reached into the back of the wagon, lifted out a large wooden toolbox with a handle on it, then headed back toward the store with Hank trailing after him like a waddling duck.

With a measuring tape, Martin calculated the expanse of the porch and made some notes with a pencil and notepad. Placing his hands on his narrow hips, he studied the wreckage. Hank copied his brother's stance, his pudgy hands on his thick waist. Standing side by side, the two brothers looked endearing. When Martin jerked on a pair of leather gloves and started stacking debris off to the side of the building, Hank did likewise.

Soon, Martin appeared at the front door. "I'm afraid the lumber is rotted clear through." He met Julia's gaze.

"What do you recommend?" she asked.

"I should install new lumber and then paint it to match the rest of the store. It'll be more sound and last you for years to come."

Again, she was struck by his self-confidence. "All right. If you'll go to the building supply store, just tell Byron Stott what you need and to put the charge on my account. I've already made arrangements with him and he knows I'll have someone coming in to buy supplies for me."

She didn't tell him that she'd also warned Byron not to let her new handyman cheat her. Byron knew he must provide her with a receipt. She'd trusted money to Dallin once and it had quickly disappeared. She wouldn't do that again.

Martin nodded, then turned on his boot heels and went outside. Hank was poking the dirt with a long stick but came running when his brother called him. As the two climbed into the buggy, Julia folded her arms, thinking it was much too cold in the shop. Soon, the snow would fly. She should speak with Martin about obtaining firewood for the old black stove. Hopefully he would know where she could buy fuel at the lowest price.

Turning, she glanced out the window, noticing the horse and buggy had disappeared from view. Trust. It wasn't a new notion to her, but something she no longer freely gave to everyone she met. Dallin had betrayed her trust, but she was willing to try one more time. She just hoped Martin Hostetler didn't let her down.

Martin stood inside the building supply store and gazed at the stacks of two-by-fours he intended to buy. Wearing his heavy leather gloves, he lifted several boards onto his flat cart and thought about the woman who had just hired him.

Julia Rose was pretty, with a small upturned nose, a stubborn chin and soft brown eyes that showed intelligence and an eagerness to succeed but also a bit of self-doubt. With her russet hair pulled back in a long ponytail and no makeup, she looked almost Amish. But not in the blue jeans and shirt she was wearing. And most definitely not without the white organdy prayer *kapp* that all Amish women wore.

She was *Englisch*. A woman of the world. Yet, Martin couldn't help admiring her spunk. The way she'd stood on that rickety ladder and gripped the hammer told him she was determined. In fact, she reminded him of his *mamm*, who had raised six children and still worked beside his *daed* after twenty-eight years, doing whatever needed to be done without complaint.

"Whatcha gonna make?" Hank asked in Deitsch, the German dialect his Amish people used among themselves.

Martin turned and found his brother standing beside him. He was as sweet and sincere as they came. The Amish only went to school through the eighth grade. Now that Hank was too old for that, Martin had taken him under his wing. Both his parents tended to lose their patience with Hank and his penchant for getting into trouble, but Martin had deep compassion for his younger brother and had recently started taking the boy with him.

"Remember, we're making a porch overhang for Rose Soapworks?" Martin said.

"*Ja*, that's right. I remember now," Hank said, his thick voice filled with a happy lilt. Nothing seemed to ruffle the boy's feathers. He was always in a good mood.

Pushing his cart, Martin headed toward the aisle where sheets of metal siding were stacked in tidy order. He was careful not to buy too much. He'd been pleasantly surprised when Julia Rose had told him to come pick out the supplies he would need and he didn't want to betray her trust.

"Julia's gonna like the porch we make, huh, Mar-tin?" Hank said, speaking his name as if it were two words.

"*Ja*, I hope so. But you should call her Miss Rose."

"How come? I like her name. Julia. Julia. Julia," Hank repeated in his heavy staccato voice.

"It's not good manners for you to call her by her first name. She's a grown woman and you're still a youth. It's proper for you to call her Miss Rose." Martin stepped past the boy, pushing his cart as he went.

With dogged determination, Hank hurried after him.

"I like her last name, too. Rose. Rose. Rose. How come she's got two first names?"

"I don't know but Rose is her last name." Martin didn't try to overexplain as he rounded the corner and quickly filled a paper sack with nails and lag bolts. He was used to his brother's incessant chatter and didn't let it bother him. He selected several pieces of flashing to sieve off water during rainstorms.

Hank grinned and slid his dirty fingers beneath the suspenders crossing his shirtfront. He'd removed his leather gloves and tucked them into his waistband. "We're gonna get enough money to build your barn, huh?"

"We're working toward that goal and a little extra so *Mamm* can make you a new coat and vest for Church Sunday," Martin conceded.

"*Ach*, a gray coat 'cause I look *gut* in gray. Julia sure is *schee*. Don't you think so?"

"Miss Rose," Martin corrected.

"*Ja*, Miss Rose sure is *schee*," Hank said.

Yes, Julia was pretty, but Martin didn't say so. It wouldn't be proper, especially since she was *Englisch*. Even now, he couldn't forget the soft feel of her during those few scant seconds when he'd held her in his arms, or the fragrance of her hair, a subtle mixture of citrus. And the moment he'd looked into her beautiful brown eyes, he'd felt something shift inside his heart like the cracking of a giant oak tree's trunk beneath a bolt of lightning.

No! He mustn't think such things. Julia wasn't Amish and he didn't want to do anything unseemly that might get him into trouble with his parents or church elders.

Hurrying to the front of the store, he set the bag of

nails on the counter. Byron Stott, the proprietor, stood behind the cash register. He pushed a jagged thatch of salt-and-pepper hair out of his eyes and glanced at Martin.

"Anything else you need?"

"*Ne*, this is all. Please put everything on Julia Rose's account," Martin said.

Byron lifted a bushy eyebrow in curiosity. "So, she hired you as her handyman, did she?"

Martin nodded.

"And me, too," Hank chimed in.

Byron grunted. "She told me someone would be coming in."

Martin stood silent. Though he had lived in this community over ten years and knew the townspeople quite well, he was Amish and understood the expectations of his faith. He should keep himself apart from the world and not become too friendly with the *Englisch* townsfolk.

Moving around Martin's cart, Byron lifted and moved each item to access the price tag. The beep of the scanning gun filled the air in quick repetition.

"You gonna ask Julia to drive home with you from the singings?" Hank asked his brother.

Noticing that Byron was watching him with amusement, Martin's face flushed with heat and he quickly turned away. "*Ne*, of course not."

The singings were usually held after church services and included all the young people who were of dating age. As a group, they spent the evening singing or, if weather permitted, playing volleyball outside. They enjoyed refreshments afterward and frequently the young men drove the young women home in their buggies.

Alone. This form of Amish dating frequently resulted in marriage. But at the age of twenty-five, Martin had long ago stopped attending such events because the girls were too young and immature to hold his interest.

"How come?" Hank persisted.

"Your kind can't marry outside your church." Byron Stott spoke as if it should be obvious.

"Oh." Hank's mouth rounded in confusion. He stared at the man, the tip of his tongue protruding between his lips. "But what if she becomes Amish? Then it would be okay. Right?"

Martin didn't respond but he saw Byron's curious stare. This wasn't the first time that Hank had embarrassed him in public.

"Since you don't want her, I'm gonna invite her to the singing. We can make her Amish and then she's gonna be my girl," Hank said in a happy voice.

Byron flipped a lever and opened the till on the cash register as he laughed out loud. "A grown woman like Julia Rose isn't gonna join the Amish and she definitely won't be your girl."

Martin bristled at the proprietor's unkind words but remained mute.

Hank scowled. "How come? I'd treat her real *gut*. Just like my *vadder* treats my *mudder*. She is his queen. And that's how I'd treat Julia. Like a queen."

Byron just snorted and looked away.

Martin didn't say a word. He didn't want to hurt his brother's feelings. *Familye* and marriage meant everything to the Amish people. Telling Hank that he would probably never marry and have a *familye* of his own wouldn't be nice.

Not when Martin had failed to secure a wife for himself. He knew he should have wed long ago. It was the expectation of his people. He'd stepped out with every eligible Amish woman here in Riverton and those living in the nearby town of Westcliffe, too. A couple of years ago, he'd spent several months with his relatives in Indiana, seeking a suitable Amish wife. But he'd failed miserably. It seemed either the woman didn't want him or he didn't want her, with nothing in between.

He thought about Julia Rose again and the way the sunlight gleamed against her russet hair. Wouldn't it be ironic if he finally found someone he wanted to marry... and she happened to be *Englisch*? Such a relationship would never work. Either Martin would be shunned for marrying outside his faith, or his wife would have to convert. He couldn't see either scenario happening between him and Julia Rose. Besides, his faith was too important for him to give up.

His thoughts were ridiculous and he almost laughed out loud at his silly musings.

Byron completed the tally, made some notes on a ledger, then handed a long receipt to Martin.

"Give this to Julia. She'll be expecting it," Byron said.

With a quick nod, Martin folded the receipt and tucked it inside his black felt hat since he had no pockets.

"*Ach*, I don't see why I can't invite Julia to the singings just because she isn't Amish. I'm gonna ask her to be my girl. You just wait and see," Hank mumbled as they headed outside.

Martin was not going to comment. Not in a million years. Hank saw mostly the good in other people and didn't always understand social mores. Although their mother was accepting of Hank's Down syndrome, she had confided to Martin once that she feared she had been punished by *Gott* for doing something wrong. Martin had comforted her, believing it was just the way Hank was. The boy was so eager to please and rarely showed anger or malice. He brought so much joy into their lives that Martin thought he was a blessing, not a punishment.

The buggy-wagon was parked off to the side where Byron Stott had constructed a hitching tether for his Amish clientele. Hank skipped along beside Martin, stopping to inspect an ant crawling across the pavement. Martin quickly loaded his purchases into the back of the wagon, waited for Hank to get inside the buggy, then took the lead lines into his hands and slapped them against the horse's back. As he turned onto the street and headed toward Rose Soapworks, he let the rhythmic clop of the horse's hooves settle his jangled nerves.

For some reason, Hank's senseless chatter upset him today. It had never bothered him before. Martin usually had a quiet heart. But somehow, meeting Julia Rose had unsettled him more than he'd realized.

He'd recently purchased sixty-five acres of fine farmland just two miles outside of town. In the spring, he planned to build a barn and raise horses and a *familye* of his own. But just one problem: he had no wife. No one to build a house for. No one to love and dote on the way he longed to do. No reason to work so hard for the land he'd just acquired. And no one to love him in return.

But he was determined to change all of that. And soon.

Chapter Two

"Who is that?"

Julia turned and found her mother standing beside her in the spacious workroom at the front of the store.

It was lunchtime and Julia was getting ready to make sandwiches when she thought perhaps she should ask her new workmen if they were hungry. Gazing out the wide windows, she'd been watching Martin and Hank tap-tapping with hammers as they rebuilt the front porch. Or rather, Martin did most of the work while Hank hopped around in a circle, chased a stray dog and laughed out loud at absolutely nothing at all.

"They're our new handymen. The man's name is Martin Hostetler and that's his younger brother Hank. Mr. Nelson recommended them to us," Julia said.

Her mother frowned. At the age of forty-four, Sharon Rose was still fairly young but she had lupus and not much stamina. Though she never wore makeup and insisted on keeping her long, graying hair pinned in a tight bun at the back of her head, she had a pretty face with soft brown eyes. Dressed like Julia in blue jeans and tennis shoes, Sharon took a deep breath and let it go.

"But they're Amish," she said.

"Yes, that surprised me, as well. But Martin rescued me when the porch canopy fell on top of me and he says that he's an experienced carpenter and plumber. Apparently, he's helped build numerous structures."

The scowl on Sharon's face deepened. "I have no doubt that's true. The Amish always help each other build their own homes and barns. But isn't there someone else you can hire?"

Julia figured Mom had acquired knowledge about the Amish sometime during her life. But her mother's doubt caused a lance of uncertainty to spear Julia's heart. She was trying so hard to be a savvy businesswoman and to keep her promise to her father. Had she made a mistake by hiring Martin without knowing more about him? No, she didn't think so.

"Not that I know of. Mr. Nelson told me he would send us one of the best carpenters in the area. He said the man would work hard and wouldn't cheat us," she said.

"That's probably true. The Amish are brutally honest. At least they have that quality going for them." Mom said the words with contempt, as though it was a failing rather than a virtue. That piqued Julia's curiosity even more. Since Dallin had lied to her on several occasions, she was glad to hear that she could trust Martin.

"How do you seem to know so much about them?" Julia asked.

Mom shrugged and continued to gaze out the filthy windows, her eyes narrowed and filled with doubt. "I knew some Amish people once. They were some of the most cruel, judgmental people I ever met. I don't want anything to do with them again."

Julia flinched. Wow. That sounded a bit harsh.

"Surely that was an isolated case. There are good and bad people in all walks of life, right?"

Mom hesitated several moments. "I suppose so."

"Besides, I've already hired Martin. I can't fire him now without just cause," Julia said.

Mom didn't reply, which wasn't odd. She was a quiet woman, keeping most of her thoughts to herself. Instead, Julia faced her mother and gave her a brief hug. "Don't worry, Mom. It's going to be fine."

Mom nodded and showed a tremulous smile. After all, she was still mourning Dad. "Yes, of course, you're right. I'm just being silly."

"Ahem, excuse me."

The two women whirled around and found Martin standing in the doorway, hat in hand.

"Oh, Martin. I want you to meet my mother, Sharon," Julia said.

"Mrs. Rose." He nodded courteously, his gaze never wavering.

Mom just looked at him with a sober expression. Julia didn't understand. It wasn't like her mother to be unkind or to disapprove of someone without knowing them first.

"Hank and I are gonna take a brief lunch break, if that's all right," Martin said.

"Yes, of course," Julia said. "In fact, I was just coming to ask if you'd like a sandwich."

"*Ne, danke.* We brought our own lunch." Without waiting for her reply, he disappeared from view.

Mom stepped closer to the door. A blast of sunlight gleamed through a small patch of glass that wasn't covered by grunge and Sharon lifted a hand to shade her eyes. She and Julia watched for a moment as Martin retrieved a red personal-size cooler from his buggy. Hank joined him as the two sat on the edge of the porch. Had Martin been so certain that Julia would hire him that he had packed a lunch? Or did he always come into town prepared?

"What's troubling you, Mom?" Julia asked.

Maybe Mom feared Martin might try to steal from them the way Dallin had done. It hadn't been much money but enough that it had made their lives more difficult. Mom had loved Dallin and Debbie, too. They'd become part of the family. Or so Julia had thought. They'd eloped just three weeks before Dad's death. Because he'd been on so much pain medication, Dad didn't know what Dallin had done. But the final blow was when he didn't even attend her father's funeral. Dallin and Debbie's betrayal had devastated her and Mom.

"No, of course not. I have no doubt he'll do a fine job. It's just that..."

"What?" Julia urged.

Sharon waved a hand and showed a wide smile. Reaching out, she caressed Julia's cheek. "Oh, it's nothing. I'm just missing your father, that's all. In the past, he always dealt with such things. But you're doing a fine job. I'm sure it'll be okay. And now, I'd better return to work. That back room isn't going to clean itself out."

"Mom, why don't you go lie down for a while? I know your joints are hurting and I don't want you to overdo it."

"I'm fine, dear." Sharon limped toward the hallway leading to the back of the building. Julia watched her go, worried about her despite her assurances.

When she looked back at Martin, Julia saw that he'd laid a clean cloth on the porch and pulled out several slices of homemade bread, ham, two golden pears and thick wedges of apple pie. After compiling the bread and meat into sandwiches, Hank eagerly picked one up and almost took a bite. Martin stopped him with a gentle hand on his arm. Without a word, Martin removed his hat and bowed his head reverently. Hank did likewise. For the count of thirty, the two held still and Julia realized they must be praying.

She envied the close sibling relationship they shared. There was something so serene about their bent heads that she felt a rash of goose bumps cover her arms. Then Martin released a breath and they began to eat. While Martin chewed thoughtfully, Hank's cheeks bulged with food and he glanced around with distraction.

At that moment, Martin looked up and saw her. Julia's face flushed with embarrassed heat. How rude of her to stand here and watch them. Yet, she couldn't move away. She felt transfixed with curiosity. Especially when Martin gave her a warm smile. With his back turned, Hank didn't notice her. Taking his sandwich, he hopped up and ran to climb the elm tree. Some unknown force caused Julia to step outside to speak with Martin.

"Um, I hope you don't think me impolite but can I ask what you were doing a few minutes ago?" she asked.

Martin tilted his head to the side and blinked in confusion. "You mean when I was working on the porch?"

She shook her head. "No, before you ate. You bowed your heads for a long time. Were you praying?"

He nodded and bit into his pear, chewed for a moment, then swallowed. "*Ja*, we always pray before a meal. To thank the Lord for His bounty and to ask a blessing on our food. Don't you do the same?"

How interesting. How quaint, yet authentic.

"No, I'm afraid not. I wasn't raised that way," she answered truthfully.

But even as she spoke, she wondered why not. It seemed so appropriate to thank God for all that He had given her. Rather than being odd, it seemed right.

She stepped nearer. "What do you say in your prayers?"

"That depends." He indicated that she should sit nearby on the porch and she did.

"On what?"

"*Ach*, sometimes we say the Lord's prayer before a meal. If there is trouble brewing at home or a special blessing we need, I often mention that to *Gott* and ask for His help. Other times, we pray at church meetings as a congregation and as a *familye*. And still other times, we say personal prayers in private. Most of our prayers are silent but they all differ, depending on their purpose and what is in my heart."

Yes, she could understand that. She'd oftentimes carried a prayer inside her heart but had never spoken one out loud. Because frankly, she didn't know how to do so.

"Do you pray often?" she asked.

"*Ja*, many times each day. Why do you ask?"

With her father's death, Mom's illness, Dallin's betrayal, financial problems and their recent move to Colorado, she'd needed to know God was nearby. To know that He was watching over them and she wasn't alone. But her prayers were always in silence, spoken within.

She shrugged. "I was just curious. I wasn't really raised with prayer in my daily life. But there are times when I speak to God in my heart."

He lifted his eyebrows. "You believe in *Gott* then?"

"Yes, I do." Giving voice to her belief deepened her conviction. That God lived and was conscious of His children now in modern times, just as He had been in ancient times. She'd never really gone to church, yet she had decided for herself that she believed in a loving creator who was conscious of her needs. But unfortunately, she knew very little about Him.

Martin flashed a gentle smile. "I often carry a prayer in my heart, as well. *Gott* is perfect and knows all things. He hears all prayers, even those we don't speak out loud. Although He doesn't always answer us on our timetable. When was the last time you prayed?"

She took a deep inhale and let it go. "Yesterday, but I prayed most the night my father died. I couldn't understand why God had abandoned us. But it's odd. Instead of anger, I felt a warmth deep within my chest and an unexplainable knowledge that God was with us even during that dark time. And Mom became sick with lupus even before Dad was diagnosed with cancer. She helps with the soap making but she can't do a lot. Still, I knew I'd find a way to take care of her. And then, a few months later, Carl Nelson called to say that my Grandpa Walt had passed away and left me this store. That's when we moved here. So it seems the Lord heard and answered my prayers after all. I just wish my father hadn't died."

Now why had she told Martin all of that? She didn't know him. Not really. Yet she had confided some deeply personal things to him. She stiffened her spine, hoping Martin didn't make fun of her.

"I'm sorry you lost your *vadder*," he said. "You and your *mudder* must have gone through a very difficult ordeal. But I'm so glad you recognize how the Lord has blessed you. I believe when we think all is lost, that is when *Gott* is testing us, to see if we will call on Him in faith or in anger. Yet, He doesn't leave us comfortless. He is always with us if we seek Him out."

Martin's words touched her heart like nothing else could. For a moment, she felt as though God truly was close to her. That He wasn't a remote, disinterested God, who was withdrawn and didn't really care about her and Mom.

"Hank, don't climb so far. *Komm* down now. It's time for us to get back to work," Martin called to his brother.

Turning her head, Julia saw that the boy was high in the elm, clinging to a heavy branch. The boy looked over at them, saw Julia and immediately scrambled down.

The enchanted moment was broken. Although she'd like nothing better, Julia realized she couldn't sit here all day chatting with Martin. She had plenty of work to do. Honestly, she was stunned that Martin was so easy to talk to.

"Well, I'd better get inside and help Mom. Thank you for answering my questions." She came to her feet, dusting off her blue jeans.

"Anytime," he said.

Hank came running, a huge smile on his face. "*Hallo*, Julia. Did you see how high I climbed?"

"Miss Rose," Martin corrected the boy with a stern lift of his eyebrows.

Hank ignored his brother, focusing on Julia. "I went higher than ever before. I could even see the top of your roof. You have a big hole up there where the shingles have blown away."

Julia blinked, then glanced at Martin. "Oh, dear. A hole in the roof? And winter is coming on."

"Don't worry. As soon as I've completed the porch, I'll take a look at it," Martin said.

"But there are so many other chores needing to be

done. I didn't even think about the roof." A feeling of helpless dread almost overwhelmed her.

"Never fear. The Lord will bless us and it'll all get done."

Martin sounded so confident. So sure of himself. So filled with conviction. She couldn't help envying his faith. His words of reassurance brought her a bit of comfort, but what if he was wrong? What if they didn't get the workroom set up in time?

She had been making single batches of soap up in the tiny kitchen of their apartment almost every evening but that would only satisfy the grand opening of their store on December 1. It would take her four weeks of making super batches of soap to satisfy her wholesale contract, and the soap required four to five weeks to cure after it was made. She must ship her orders by the end of January in order to meet her next contract deadline the first of February. So much was riding on her being able to make soap by the end of November. By the end of December, she had to have most of the soap made.

As she went inside, Julia hoped Martin was right.

The pressure was on. Martin knew Julia was worried. He could see it in her eyes. He'd heard the urgency in her voice and could feel the apprehension emanating from her like a living thing. If Hank was right and there was a big hole in the roof, it would need to be repaired before the autumn rains began, which was any day now. Depending on what needed to be done, it could suck up precious time he needed to build the shelves and countertops for her workroom.

It was Martin's job to get it all done in time for her to open her shop. He felt the seriousness of the situation as though his own livelihood depended on it. His reputation was on the line. He'd been doing a lot of carpentry work for people in the community and wanted to increase his business as a side job for more income to build his barn and, one day, his new house. He also wanted to make Julia happy and ease her load in any way possible.

Working as fast as he could, he built the framework of the awning first. Standing on the rickety ladder, he affixed the lag bolts. Satisfied with his labors, he looked down at Hank, who had wandered over to peer through the store windows. No doubt he was looking for Julia.

"Hank!"

The boy jerked, looking guilty. Martin resisted the urge to smile.

"Hand me up those two-by-six boards," he called.

Hank lifted a four-by-six board instead.

"*Ne*, that's the wrong one. I need the two-by-six." Martin forced himself to speak gently, although he felt impatient for his brother's mistake. It was costing him precious time.

Hank laid a hand on the smaller boards and looked up at him with a questioning gaze.

"*Ja*, those are the right ones. That's *gut*. Hand them up."

Martin reached out a hand as Hank lifted the boards one by one so he could nail them into place. By the time he'd laid the furring strips over top of the frame, it was almost dinnertime. He'd accomplished a lot today but should soon start for home. *Mamm* would be expecting them. He would finish up tomorrow. The weather should hold for a couple more days so he could repair the roof. For now, it was time to leave.

"You've done a fine job today."

He turned and saw Julia standing off to the side of the porch, looking up at him. Hank immediately raced over to stand beside her, gazing at her with adulation.

"I helped," Hank said.

She blessed him with a smile so bright that Martin had to blink. "Of course you did."

Hank beamed at her. "Do you like to sing?"

Martin stiffened, knowing what his brother was about to ask. "Not now, Hank."

Hank threw a disgruntled glare at his older brother. "But I want to ask her—"

"It's not the right time," Martin said.

Julia hesitated, looking back and forth between the two. In a bit of confusion, she spoke to Martin as she inspected his work with a critical eye. "I didn't expect you to get the porch finished today, but it looks almost complete."

"*Ja*, it has come together well. I'll put on the finishing touches and paint it first thing in the morning. I hope it is satisfactory," he said.

"It's more than satisfactory. It's beautiful. If I didn't know better, I would say it was never damaged. You've cleaned up every bit of mess, too. I can't even tell you worked on it today."

As her gaze scanned the porch and awning, he could see her searching for any imperfections. He climbed down and set the ladder aside for his use tomorrow.

"My *daed* taught me to tidy up after work," he said.

She tilted her head. "Your dat?"

"*Ja*, my dad."

"Oh, your father," she said.

"*Ja*, my *vadder*."

He'd swept up the sawdust and discarded nails and

placed them in a large garbage can. *Mamm* told him that his fastidiousness was bothersome to some of the Amish girls, which was one reason they didn't want to marry him. But instead of being irritated by his meticulous work, Julia seemed to approve. For some crazy reason, that delighted Martin like nothing else could.

She nodded with satisfaction. "I do like it very much. With a coat of paint, it'll look perfect."

While Julia watched, he packed his tools away in the toolbox. When he was finished, he faced her again. "We'd better get going. We'll see you in the morning."

"Yes, see you tomorrow." She waved and turned away, going back inside.

Martin climbed into the buggy with Hank and directed the horse toward the main road. He'd worked hard today, yet he didn't feel tired. No, not at all. Instead, he felt rejuvenated and eager to do a good job for Julia Rose.

When he pulled into the graveled driveway at home, his father was just coming from the barn, carrying two buckets of frothy white milk. His mother, sisters and other brother had just finished feeding the chickens and pigs.

"Martin! Hank! You're finally home." His mother waved, a huge smile on her cheery face.

Emily, Susan and Timmy came running, surrounding him and Hank as they hopped up and down with excitement.

"Did you get the job?" thirteen-year-old Emily asked, her face alight with expectation.

"You must have got the job because you've been gone all day," little eight-year-old Timmy reasoned.

Martin laughed as he swung seven-year-old Susan high into the air. The girl squealed with delight. Their greeting warmed his heart. How he loved them all. He thought about Julia having only her mother to come home to. It must be so lonely for her.

"Supper's about ready. *Komm* inside and tell us about your day." His father stepped up on the porch, his words silencing the children's incessant questions. At the age of forty-nine, David was the patriarch of the home and still strong and muscular from working long hours of manual labor.

"I'll just put the road horse in his stall and toss him some hay," Martin said.

Linda, his mother, waved an impatient hand. As the matriarch of the *familye*, she was just as confident in her role as David was. "*Ne*, Timmy can do that. You and Hank *komm* inside now. I want to hear all about your day."

"Ah, don't say anything important while I'm gone," Timmy called. But the boy obediently took hold of the horse's halter and led him into the barn.

Once they were inside, they washed and sat down at the spacious table in the kitchen. *Mamm* had already laid out the plates and utensils. The room was warm and smelled of something good cooking on the stove. With six hungry children and a husband to feed, Linda always made plenty. Only Martin's nineteen-year-old sister, Karen, was missing. She was newly married and lived back east with her husband.

"*Ach*, did you get the job?" His father sat down and looked at him expectantly.

"*Ja*, we got the job," Hank answered for him. The boy beamed with eagerness and Martin didn't have the heart to scold him for speaking out of turn. After all, the job was his, too.

Martin smiled with tolerance and purposefully waited until Timmy returned from the barn before speaking. Because they prayed before eating, they had to wait for the boy anyway.

Once everyone was assembled, David beckoned to his wife. "*Mudder, komm* and sit."

David pointed at her chair and Martin watched as his mother sat at the opposite end of the table, nearest the stove. As each member of the *familye* bowed their head to bless the food, he couldn't help loving this nightly ritual. His mom was always up and buzzing around the table to see to everyone's needs. But during evening prayer, she sat reverently with her *familye* for these few minutes while they gave thanks to the Lord.

When they were finished, everyone dug in and she hopped up to pull a pan of fresh-baked cornbread from the oven.

"Hank and I will be doing handyman work." Martin speared two pork chops and laid them on his plate. The clatter of utensils and eating filled the room, but no one spoke as they waited to hear every word he said.

"What kind of handyman work?" David asked as he spread golden butter across a hot piece of cornbread.

Martin sliced off a piece of meat and popped it into his mouth. He chewed for several moments before swallowing, then explained his tasks and asked his father's advice on how to assemble the cabinets in Julia's workroom. The conversation bounced around various topics but kept coming back to his new job.

"Julia's nice, too. She's real *schee*." Hank spoke with his mouth full of cooked carrots.

David's bushy eyebrows shot up and he looked at Martin. "Julia?"

"*Ja*, Julia Rose. She's my new boss," Martin said. "She lives with her *mudder* in that old building Walter Rose owned. Apparently, Julia was his granddaughter. It seems that old Walt died a couple months back and left the place to her. She's renovating it so she can sell handmade soap."

"Soap?" David said the word abruptly, like it didn't make sense.

Martin shrugged and took a long drink of fresh milk. "*Ja*, she sells it to stores across the nation."

"Humph, I guess the *Englisch* don't make their own so they have to buy it somewhere," David said. "But I thought you'd be working for a man. How old is this Julia?"

Martin took a deep breath, trying to answer truthfully while not alarming his father. After all, it wasn't seemly that an unmarried Amish man should be working for a young, attractive *Englisch* woman. "She's twenty-three but she stays in the house most of the time while Hank and I work outside. The job is only for six or seven weeks, so it'll be over with soon enough."

His father's gaze narrowed and rested on him like a ten-ton sledge. Martin felt as though the man were looking deep inside of him for the truth. Linda also paused in front of the counter where she was slicing big wedges of cherry pie. She didn't say anything, waiting for her husband's verdict on this turn of events, but Martin could tell from her expression that she was worried.

"*Ach*, I guess you've got Hank with you all the time, so you're not alone with this woman," David finally said. "And once it's done, you'll have enough money to build your barn in the spring. But don't forget who you

are and what *Gott* expects from you, *sohn*. Always remember your faith."

"I will," Martin assured him.

"But she's *Englisch*. Are you sure this is wise?" Linda
asked, her brow furrowed in a deep frown.

"*Mamm*, don't worry," Martin reassured her with a
short laugh. "I'm a grown man and know how to handle
myself. Besides, it's only for a short time. It isn't as if
I'm going to fall in love and leave our faith or something
crazy like that, so rest your fears."

"And besides, Julia's gonna be my *maedel*, not Martin's," Hank said.

David and Linda shared a look of concern, to which
Martin quickly explained the boy's desire for Julia to be
his girl. "I've already told Hank that Julia isn't Amish
and she's too old for him anyway."

Without missing a beat, Martin's sister Emily handed
him a bowl of boiled potatoes. Martin forked several
onto his plate. The whole *familye* knew the drill, having
discussed issues like this a zillion times before.

"Why does it matter if Julia isn't Amish?" Hank
asked with a frown.

Linda shook her head and shooed Hank's question
away with her hand. "She's not of our faith. She's not
one of us." Handing plates of pie to Emily to pass around
the table, she leaned against the counter and faced Martin again. "So, tell us something about this woman boss
of yours."

Taking a bite of buttered potato, Martin kept his voice
slow and even, trying not to say anything that might
overly alarm his mother. "She and her *mudder* live a
simple life like us. They don't wear makeup or fancy
clothes. Nor do they own a car or use electricity. Julia

has even asked me a couple of questions about our faith. And she's devoted to her *mudder*, who is sickly."

Linda winced with sympathy. "What's wrong with her?"

"She has lupus. Julia's father recently died of cancer. Julia's been earning a living for them and taking care of her parents. From what I can see, she's a *gut*, hard-working woman."

"But she's not Amish," David said, his bushy eyebrows raised in a stern look that allowed for no more discussion on the matter.

Linda stepped near and rested a hand on Martin's shoulder. "*Ach*, you'll be careful not to be drawn in by her, won't you, *sohn*? I couldn't bear to lose you. You'll remember what your *vadder* and I have taught you and stay true to your faith."

He met his mother's eyes, his convictions filling his heart. He could never stand to hurt her by chasing after an *Englisch* woman. "You don't need to worry about me, *Mamm*. I will only marry someone of our faith. This I vow."

"*Gut*. It's too bad you can't convert Julia to our faith." Linda showed a smile of relief and finally sat down to eat her own supper. The conversation turned to what the younger children were learning in school.

Martin ate his meal, listening to the chatter around him. He'd done his best to alleviate his parents' concerns but knew they were worried. And he agreed that it was too bad Julia wasn't Amish. If she were, his parents would have no reservations about him working with her.

As he carried his dishes over to the sink for washing, he listened to Hank's incessant chatter and a feeling of expectancy built within his chest. He couldn't wait to return to work in the morning and be near Julia again. And though he refused to consider the options, he knew deep inside that it had little to do with the money he would earn and more to do with his pretty employer.

But he meant what he'd said. He would marry an Amish woman or not at all.

Chapter Three

The following morning, Julia glanced at the clock she'd hung on the wall in her spacious workroom. She blinked, hardly able to believe it was barely five o'clock. She'd been up for two hours already. Like many mornings, she couldn't sleep, so she'd started work early.

After she completed several tasks, faint sunlight filtered through the dingy windows, highlighting the bare wooden floors with streamers of dust. She really must wash the windows today, before she painted the walls. That should brighten things up quite a bit. With the delays from yesterday, she feared Martin might not have time for everything needing to be done. Careful not to let Mom work too hard, Julia had helped her clear most of the boxes and junk out of the room, stacking them in the backyard. Above all, her priority was to get the soap room operational. But a hole in the roof could create worse problems down the road.

Squinting her eyes, she worked by kerosene light. She'd acquired an old stainless steel sink from the discount store in town and wanted it ready once Martin built the cabinets she required. Using a mild cleanser, she scrubbed at a particularly grimy spot. The sink's two spacious tubs would accommodate the big pots she used for soap making.

Martin would be here in a few hours to finish the porch. Then he'd check the condition of the roof. After that, she wanted him to—

Tap-tap-tap.

She looked up, thinking the sound came from above. Had Mom awakened early and was doing something inside their apartment? She caught the deep timbre of a man's voice coming from outside but wasn't sure. It came again, followed by Hank's unique accent. She glanced at the wall clock and discovered it was almost eight. Ah, her handymen were already here and the sun was barely up.

"Be careful with that paint, Hank. You don't want to spill any." Martin's muffled voice reached her ears.

Sitting back, Julia set aside the soft sponge. In her warm slippers, she padded over to the window and peered out.

Martin and Hank stood side by side in front of the porch as they perused their handiwork. Each of them held a brush that gleamed with white paint. Martin also clutched the handle of a paint bucket. No doubt they'd been trimming the porch and front of the building. A feeling of elation swept over Julia. She couldn't wait for it all to be finished.

Martin had rolled the long sleeves of his shirt up his muscular arms. A smear of white paint marred his angular chin. Hank also wore several smatters of paint on his forearms and clothes. In the early morning sunlight, Julia caught the gleam of bright trim on the post nearest to the window but couldn't see the rest of the porch from this angle. And all that work had been done while she was cleaning the new sink.

Hmm. Dallin had never worked this hard. He'd rather laze around and borrow money from Julia, which he never paid back. Maybe it was a blessing she hadn't married him after all.

Walking over to the front door, she flipped the dead bolt, turned the knob and stepped out onto the porch. In that short amount of time, Martin had climbed to the top of the rickety ladder leading up to the roof. Hank held the ladder steady from below. Busy with their labors, they hadn't noticed her yet. She watched as Martin dipped his brush into a bucket of paint he'd set on the pail shelf, then touched up a spot high on the side of the awning. As he concentrated on his work, he pressed the tip of his tongue against his upper lip.

The ladder trembled.

"Hold it steady, Hank. Just a few more spots and we'll be finished. Then we can start on the roof." Martin spoke without looking down.

Fearing she might break his concentration, Julia didn't say anything. A tabby cat crossing the road caught Hank's attention. Julia knew the animal was named Tigger and belonged to Essie Walkins, the elderly widow who lived two houses down. Tail high in the air, the feline picked its way across the abandoned street. No doubt it was hoping to cajole Julia out of a bowl of milk. She'd fed the cat many times, much to her mother's chagrin. Sharon didn't like strays.

Seeing the feline, Hank abandoned his post and hurried toward Tigger. Without the boy's weight to hold the ladder steady, it shuddered uncontrollably.

Julia gasped as Martin grabbed on to the gutter to

keep from falling. She rushed over and gripped the sides of the ladder, staring up at him with widened eyes. The ladder stabilized but too late. The bucket of paint plummeted to the ground with a heavy thud. Julia scrunched her shoulders, hoping she wouldn't get hit in the head by the falling object. Spatters of white struck the outer wall of the building, the mass of paint pooling in the middle of the wooden porch.

"Oh, no!" Julia breathed in exasperation.

Martin stared down at her with absolute shock. Likewise, Julia was so stunned that she was held immobile for several seconds. Then, Martin hurried down the ladder, his angular face torn by an expression of dread.

"*Ach*, Julia! Are you all right? The bucket didn't hit you, did it?" He rested a gentle hand on her arm, his dark eyes filled with concern as he searched her expression.

She shook her head. "No, it missed me. I'm fine."

Satisfied she was okay, Martin stepped away. She could still feel the warmth of his strong fingers tingling against her skin. As he perused the mess, his lips tightened. Then, his gaze sought out his recalcitrant brother.

Hank stood in the middle of the vacant street, clutching the tabby cat close against his chest as he stroked the animal's furry head. Tigger looked completely content as the boy walked over to them, smiling wide with satisfaction.

"*Ach*, look at this *bussli*. Isn't she beautiful? I saved her from being hit by a car," the boy crowed, his eyes sparkling.

"Him," Julia corrected. "The cat's name is Tigger and he's a boy."

Hank's expression lit up with sheer pleasure. "*Ach*, Tigger. What a fine name."

"Hank, there are no cars coming at this time of the morning. You were supposed to be holding the ladder for me, not chasing after *die katz*." Martin's voice held a note of reproach but was otherwise calm. He wore a slight frown, doing an admirable job of controlling his temper. In that moment, Julia respected Martin even more.

"I know, but I saw Tigger and didn't want him to get hit by a *kaer*," Hank said.

Julia glanced at the empty street. Since it was so early, there wasn't a single car, truck or person in sight. But being an agricultural community, Julia knew that would soon change as farmers came into town early to transact their business. Since Tigger freely roamed the streets at all hours of the day, she wasn't too worried he'd be struck by a car.

"You know how fast motor vehicles go," Hank continued. "Remember what happened to Jeremiah Beiler last year when an *Englischer*'s car hit his buggy-wagon and broke his leg? It nearly kilt him and his *dechder*."

"Killed, not kilt," Martin corrected the boy.

"His deck-der?" Julia asked, confused by some of their foreign words.

"Daughters," Martin supplied. "They were riding with him in the buggy when the car struck them from behind."

"Oh," Julia said.

"*Ach*, I couldn't let this sweet kitty get hurt." Hank nuzzled Tigger's warm fur, completely oblivious that his efforts to protect the cat had endangered his brother's life and created a big mess that would now have to be cleaned up.

Meeting Martin's frustrated expression, Julia showed

an understanding smile. "It's okay. No harm was done. We'll just tidy it up."

Martin rested his hands on his lean hips and gazed at the splattered paint with resignation. He certainly wasn't a man who angered easily. That was another difference between him and Dallin. Julia's ex-fiancé had raised his voice at her numerous times while kicking things and slamming doors. She hadn't liked it one bit. In retrospect, she was so grateful he was out of her life. But who would she marry now? Would there ever be a kind, hardworking man for her to love? She wasn't sure she'd ever be able to trust another man.

"How exactly do we clean up the paint?" she asked, wondering if a thinner from the hardware store might remove the white stain from the wood.

"You don't need to do a thing. I'll get this straightened out as fast as I can and reimburse you for the waste," Martin promised.

Again, she was impressed by his integrity. "There's no need for reimbursement. The porch is all but finished and it doesn't look like we lost much paint. In fact, everything looks great, except for the spill. Let me help you clean it up." She reached for a bucket of rags sitting near the front door, grateful when Martin didn't refuse her aid.

While Hank snuggled the cat, they shoveled the drying pool of paint into a heavy-duty plastic bag and set it in the waste bin to be disposed of later. Julia held the dustpan for Martin, wondering how they would get the streaks of white off the wooden porch. Since Martin was so good at his job, she decided to let him handle the problem.

"You're up early," Martin spoke as they worked.

Julia smiled. "I was thinking the same about you. There's no need for you and Hank to come to work so early."

He shrugged. "We're always up early. I usually milk the cows and feed the horses before the sun rises. I had my chores at home finished and decided to get an early start here. I'm determined to repair your roof by the end of the day, although I didn't expect this added chore."

He chuckled and Julia stared. She thought the Amish were a very stern, serious people. She had no idea they laughed and was glad he found the situation amusing. After all, her mother had taught her there was no use crying over spilled milk. It was better to just clean it up and move on. It seemed that Martin was of the same inclination.

She laughed, too, suddenly so grateful he was here. Since her broken engagement and her father's death, she'd felt so alone in the world. It was nice to have someone capable to depend on.

"Well, accidents are bound to happen now and then," she said.

"You're very understanding."

He stood to his full height and she gazed up into his eyes. With the early morning sunlight gleaming at his back, it highlighted his red hair and seemed to accent the shadows of his handsome face. She was caught there, mesmerized for several moments. Then, she mentally shook herself. After all, Martin was Amish and she wasn't. They could never be more than friends. It was that simple.

"How will we clean the wood siding?" she asked, forcing herself to look away.

"I believe I have some sand paper in my toolbox. If

I'm careful, I can take off just the bare layer of paint without damaging the wood and no one will know it was ever there." He indicated the box sitting nearby.

Opening the lid, he pulled out a sheet of gritty paper and a hand sander. While Julia swept up the dust, he sanded the porch just enough to get the paint off. The work delayed them by an hour but Martin didn't say a word when it came time to climb up and check the roof.

"Martin, I'm grateful for your dedication, but I'd like to suspend your next task for thirty minutes, please," Julia said.

Poised at the bottom of the ladder, his forehead furrowed in a quizzical frown. "What do you need me to do?"

She smiled, resting a hand on the side of the ladder so near to his own. "I think it's time we retire this rickety old thing. Would you mind going to the supply store and purchasing a good, solid ladder that will ensure our safety?"

A low chuckle rumbled inside his chest and she stared, mesmerized by the sound.

"*Ja*, I'd be happy to do that. I'll go and hurry right back," he said. "Come on, Hank."

He stepped away from the porch, tugging on Hank's arm to get the boy to follow him.

"But I want to stay here with Tigger." The boy stuck out his chin, refusing to release his hold on the cat.

"If it would make things easier for you, Hank can wait here with me. He can help me fix breakfast," Julia offered. Surely Hank wouldn't get into as much trouble if he remained behind, and Martin would be quicker with his errand, too.

"We have already eaten at home. Our *mamm* fixed us a big breakfast before we left," Martin said.

"Then perhaps Hank can help me finish cleaning out the workroom. I'm going to paint the walls today," she said.

Martin hesitated, a doubtful expression on his face. "You're certain you don't mind watching him while I'm gone? He can be a bit of a handful at times."

She waved Martin on. "Of course. We'll see you in a while."

Turning toward Hank, she indicated that the boy should follow her. "Come on, Hank. Let's go upstairs and see if we can get a bowl of milk for Tigger."

"*Ja*, I'm sure he's hungry," Hank said.

Smiling happily, the teenager followed her inside, carrying Tigger with him. Julia didn't look back to see if Martin was still watching her, but she didn't have to. She could feel his gaze resting on her like a leaden weight. And as she led Hank upstairs, she wasn't sure why her chest felt all warm and buoyant inside.

Martin was gone a total of twenty minutes. Driving his horse and buggy, he pulled up in front of the supply store and whipped inside to peruse the selection of ladders. After choosing one that was sturdy but not too costly, he asked Byron Stott to put it on Julia's account, then hurried back to Rose Soapworks.

He didn't disturb Julia to find out where Hank was. Hoping to get some work done, he set the new ladder against the side of the house and scrambled up to the rooftop with his tool belt strapped around his waist. Bracing himself so he wouldn't fall, he sat against the chimney and analyzed the problem. Sure enough, there was a hole in the roof. Not too bad. The tar paper and shingles had blown off and the wood beneath was starting to rot away. Martin knew he could fix it with little effort. And while he was up here, he'd replace the missing shingles in other areas before they became a bigger problem, too. When he was through, Julia's roof would be ready to face winter.

Using the claw of his hammer, he pried up the decayed fragments and tossed them over the side of the house where they fell harmlessly to the ground below. Wouldn't Julia be surprised when he finished the project by midday? Then he could build the shelves in her workroom.

"Martin?"

He jerked, startled from his task. Julia stood at the top of the ladder, holding on to the edge of the roof. Her eyes were wide and anxious, her face drawn with worry.

Something was wrong.

"You shouldn't be up here. You might fall," he said, wondering why he cared so much.

She blinked. "I… I need to speak with you on an urgent matter. It's about Hank. Could you come down, please?"

Oh, no. What had Hank done now? Martin hated to think ill of his younger brother but feared the boy may have done something bad during his absence.

"*Ja.* I'll climb down now."

Her head and shoulders disappeared from view. Moving carefully, Martin scooted over to the eave so he could grasp the top of the ladder and place his booted feet on the rungs. Julia had already scampered to the bottom and was looking up at him expectantly. Climbing down, he stood next to her. One glance at her ashen face told him that she was quite upset. She wrung her hands in front of her, her movements increasing his own urgency.

"What is it? What's wrong?" he asked.

"It's Hank. He...he's missing," she said.

Missing!

A flush of dismay swept over Martin. This wasn't the first time Hank had taken off by himself. Usually it was harmless and they found him easily. But once, the boy had gotten himself so lost that it took a day and night with the entire *Gmay* searching to find him. Still, Martin didn't want to panic needlessly.

Taking a deep, settling breath, he held out a calming hand. "First, tell me what happened."

"I... I don't know," Julia said. "We were upstairs in the kitchen with Mom and I was getting a bowl of milk for Tigger. One minute, Hank was there with us and the next minute, he was gone. We've searched everywhere. Upstairs, downstairs and even outside. We can't find him."

"Don't worry. We'll find him. Can you show me where you last saw him?" he asked, determined not to give in to the alarm coursing through his body.

"Come with me." She hurried toward the front door and he followed as she swept through the spacious workroom, down a long hallway to the back of the building and then hurried up a flight of stairs to the apartment above.

Once inside, Martin removed his hat, his heavy boots thudding against the bare wood floors. The landing upstairs opened into a small but comfortable living area. The spacious rugs covering the floors looked clean but threadbare. Sharon Rose stood before the kitchen sink, holding a dish towel as she dried a plate. Tigger sat on the floor nearby, his tail curled around him as he sat licking his paws in smooth, languid motions. An empty bowl rested beside the cat and Martin figured Tigger had already lapped up his milk.

Martin nodded a respectful greeting to Sharon. "*Hallo*, Mrs. Rose."

"Hello, Martin." The woman didn't smile and spoke rather stiffly before turning to reach for another plate in the dish drain.

He didn't have time to consider why Mrs. Rose didn't seem to like him. Maybe the woman was just nervous having strangers in her home.

"May I take a quick look around?" he asked Julia.

She released a pensive sigh. "Of course. Maybe you can find him."

With Julia tagging along behind, he called for his brother as he headed toward the back bedrooms. "Hank! It's Martin. Where are you?"

Embarrassed to be wandering through Julia's home, he peered behind each door and under each bed. The furnishings were sparse and excruciatingly tidy. Except for an occasional clock or picture of a landscape hanging on the walls, the rooms were devoid of all the worldly clutter that invaded so many *Englisch* homes.

As if sensing his thoughts, Julia gave a nervous cough. "We didn't bring much with us from Kansas. We sold all but the necessities."

Martin nodded, hating to invade Julia and her mother's privacy like this. Her comment gave him a bit of insight into what they'd been through. He imagined losing her father and moving to another state hadn't been easy on them. In fact, he remembered when his own *familye* had moved here over ten years ago. He'd been fifteen years of age. Old enough to wonder if his father's plan to start over in a strange place with little water for their crops and a short growing season might be a huge mistake. But it had worked out. His family was happy and doing well. If only he could find a good Amish woman to marry and start a family of his own, his life would be perfect.

"You see? There's no sign of him. It's like he just disappeared." Standing in front of a narrow walk-in closet, Julia lifted her hands in dismay.

"Maybe he is outside."

Julia shook her head. "I don't think so. The stairs creak and I'm certain I would have heard him go down. He must still be up here but I don't know where."

"May I look behind your clothes? Once, Hank hid beneath a quilt in an armoire. He could be hiding anywhere," he said.

"Yes. Whatever it takes." Julia stepped aside.

He slid the closet door open and reached in to push the clothes away. A panel of wood with a latch affixed at the top was set into the back wall… A small doorway.

"That's just the crawl space up to the attic. It's quite dark in there. Surely he wouldn't have gone inside?"

Martin shrugged. "I'm not so sure. I've learned from past experience not to bypass any possibility."

"Oh. Well, I haven't been in there yet, though I've been meaning to check it out once the electricity is turned back on. The door is still closed. Wouldn't it be open if Hank had gone in?" Julia asked.

"Who knows?" Martin said.

Without asking permission, he tugged on the pull and the panel swung open. It had a knob on the inside, which would make it easy to close. As he hunkered down, Martin was conscious of Julia joining him in the bottom of the closet. She crouched beside him, so close that her shoulder brushed against his arm and her sweet, clean fragrance filled his nose.

Peering inside, Martin blinked to adjust his eyes to the dim interior. Just beyond the doorway, a stair with a splintered handrail led up to the attic. Scrunching his shoulders so he could fit past the slim doorway, he climbed the few steps, conscious of Julia following. The railing wobbled, the stairway narrow and rickety.

"Be careful on these stairs. They feel like they're about to give way. It might be best if you wait here," he told Julia.

She nodded, staying where she was. He figured he'd have to rebuild the stairs when he had more time.

The attic was cramped and he had to stoop over because of his great height. As the room opened into view, he saw the skeletal structure of bare rafters intersected with gray sheets of insulation. No plywood had been laid across the beams of lumber so that a person could walk safely across the room. The thin drywall that made up the floor also provided the false ceiling for the apartment below but it wouldn't support much weight. A heavy layer of dust covered the entire room. Vague sunlight gleamed through a vent set high in the outside wall.

"Hank! *Ben je er?*" he called loudly.

A faint whimper came from across the expanse of the room. Glancing into the shadows, Martin saw his brother huddled in a far corner, his face contorted with fear. He must have walked across the rafters. Otherwise, he could have fallen through the floor to the apartment below.

"Mar-tin," the boy whispered, as though he didn't dare speak any louder.

"Hank!"

"Oh, he's here! I'm so glad," Julia breathed the words with amazement.

Relief flooded Martin. He'd found his brother. Hank was safe. "What are you doing in here? Could you not hear us calling you? Why have you not come out?"

He spoke in Deitsch, trying to keep his voice calm in spite of the irritation coursing through his veins.

An expression of guilt crossed the boy's features. "I… I feared you might be angry with me for coming up here."

Martin took a deep inhale and let it go. His poor, sweet brother. Did he not understand how much he loved him? A spear of compassion pierced Martin's heart. Right now, he just wanted Hank out of here and on safe ground.

"*Ne*, I am not angry," he spoke gently. "It was wrong for you to *komm* here and you must not do it again but no harm has been done. Now, take my hand."

Martin stepped out onto one of the strong rafters and lifted his arm, waiting for his brother to move toward him.

Hank stood away from the wall, holding onto the beams of timber that stretched overhead. As the boy did so, he walked on the narrow beams crisscrossing the floor like a gymnast negotiating the balance beams. Unfortunately, Hank was not light on his feet and tottered on the narrow boards. Losing his balance, he stepped on the insulation and his foot promptly crashed through the flimsy flooring.

Julia gasped, her body going tense.

"Hank!" Martin yelled.

The boy sprawled among the scratchy insulation. He

wrapped his arms around one of the strong floor planks, his left leg disappearing below.

"Hold on. I'll *komm* to you," Martin said.

A feeling of dread pulsed through his veins as he stepped out onto the narrow joists. He had no idea how solid the timbers were and didn't want Hank to fall through to the apartment below.

"Be careful." Julia spoke the warning softly, but there was no need. Martin's senses were on high alert as he crossed to his brother.

Reaching out, Martin pulled Hank up, careful not to jerk on the boy's leg and cut him on the jagged pieces of drywall. Like a little child, Hank wrapped his arms around Martin's waist and pushed his face against his chest as he held on tight.

"Mar-tin, I fell," Hank cried, his eyes wide with terror, his voice vibrating with tears.

"*Ja*, but you're all right now. Step only on the beams of lumber. They are strong. The insulation is supported only by drywall and won't hold your weight," Martin warned.

Within moments, he had Hank back at the stairway and Julia pulled the boy into the safety of the closet. She hugged him tight.

"Oh, I'm so glad you're all right. I was so worried about you," she told the boy.

Hank gave a startled laugh. "*Ja*, me, too."

"Thank the Lord you're all right," Martin said.

"Mar-tin, you saved me," Hank said, clutching his brother.

"Is he okay?"

Martin turned and saw Sharon standing in the bedroom, her eyes wide with concern.

"*Ja*, he is fine," Martin said.

"Good, that's all that matters. But now we have another small problem. There is a big hole in my bedroom where Hank's foot came through the ceiling," the woman said.

Martin froze, hardly able to believe what he heard. Oh, no. Because of Hank, it seemed he now had another repair job to rectify. Maybe it hadn't been such a good idea to bring Hank along with him on this project. It seemed he just created more work.

Stealing a quick glance at Julia, Martin tried to gauge her expression. Hopefully she wouldn't fire him on the spot. But her face was curved into a smile. And then she started to laugh. A high, lilting sound that caused a warming pleasure to flood Martin's chest.

"This day seems full of surprises. What else could go wrong?" she asked, her shoulders shaking with amusement.

Sharon smiled, too, but then seemed to catch herself. With a frowning glare tossed at Martin, she turned and walked out of the room.

"Shall we go take a look at the latest development?" Julia asked Hank.

The boy nodded and she took his hand. He held on tight, seeming perfectly happy to be in her company. Martin couldn't believe how kind and forgiving she was. Some of the Amish women he'd hoped to marry had barely tolerated Hank and his chaotic ways. He was too much work for them. The fact that Hank constantly wanted to be with Martin was a big deterrent for him being able to find a suitable bride. But Julia didn't seem to mind the boy at all. In fact, she welcomed him with humor and grace.

"There is one thing I've learned today," Julia called over her shoulder as she headed down the hallway with Hank in tow.

"And what is that?" Martin asked.

"The attic would make a great hiding place. As long as we don't fall through the rafters, that is." She laughed again.

"*Ja*, now I know where to walk, it'd be a *gut* place for me to hide. I just have to step on the rafters, not on the insulation," Hank said.

"*Ne*, you must not go up there again," Martin said.

"I won't. There are spiders in there." The boy gave a shiver of revulsion.

Again, Julia's laughter rang through the air. Martin stopped for a moment and watched her. She was unlike any woman he'd ever met. In the past, he'd thought all women were the same. One was pretty much just like all the rest. But now, he knew he'd been utterly wrong. Because he'd never met anyone quite like Julia Rose.

Chapter Four

A week later, Julia studied the swatches of colors and cabinet stains laid out in front of her, surprised by the number of choices Martin had provided. For an Amish man, he seemed quite versatile and she felt a tad overwhelmed by her options.

"I wouldn't recommend white for your workroom. It's too light and will show every bit of grime. Over time, your cabinets would start to look dingy. But white might look nice in your store," Martin said.

Standing beside her in the workroom, he pointed at one of the sample strips she held in her hands. Hank was upstairs in the kitchen with Sharon, who was baking cinnamon rolls.

"Oak or maple might be better for your workroom," Martin said.

"Yes, I agree," Julia said. "But there are so many styles to choose from. This beveling would be beautiful, but I don't need fancy cupboards. It's a workroom, after all. Soap making can be a messy job, no matter how tidy I try to keep things."

He nodded and reached out to touch one of the samples. "This one is quite modest and not too expensive. I can put pulls on each drawer and cabinet, to make it easier to open them."

She wholeheartedly agreed. It seemed their tastes were similar. "Yes, let's go with this plain style and the oak finish for the workroom and the white for the retail part of the store."

A smile of approval curved his handsome mouth. "That's exactly what I would choose. I can start building the cabinets today."

She wasn't surprised. Martin worked fast. In spite of the mishaps over the past week, he'd repaired the roof and the hole in the attic from where Hank had fallen through. And just in time, too. As soon as he finished, they had awoken to leaden clouds and a drenching rain. Julia figured Martin and Hank wouldn't show up for work today. After all, they had to drive their horse and buggy three miles into town. But they'd shown up promptly at six o'clock, wearing shiny black water slickers to protect them from the wet drizzle.

"I've been meaning to ask if you know where I might purchase some firewood. My grandfather left me a little money, so I can pay for it. Is there a vendor in town who sells it?" she asked, leaning her hip against the table she'd placed along one wall to set papers on. Martin had provided a rather orderly drawing of blueprints and designs for her workroom and they had discussed a few changes to the layout.

"*Ja*, I can see to it. We're late in the season for gathering firewood but I'll plan an excursion into the mountains to gather dead trees and haul them down to cut up for you within the next week or so," he said.

Hmm. He didn't need another chore to do. But he

never flinched at any of her many requests. Dallin had always shirked her appeals for help. But Martin seemed to understand the needs were real and simply figured out a way to accomplish each task. She couldn't help wondering if that might end once the newness of working for her wore off.

"Do you think you'll have time for that along with everything else I've asked you to do?" she said.

He nodded, rolling up the designs with quick twists of his strong hands. "*Ja.* The day after tomorrow might be a *gut* day to go up on the mountain. Tomorrow is Sunday and the weather should be clear by Monday. I can get the cabinets started today and then bring down a load of firewood next week."

She studied him for a moment, thinking. "And what about the garbage piled out back? How do we get rid of that?"

"On my way into the mountains, I can take all the boxes and junk to the dump. That way, I can kill two ducks with one stone," he said.

She laughed. "I think you mean kill two *birds* with one stone."

He smiled and tilted his head in agreement. "*Ja*, that is what I meant. I'll bring my *vadder*'s large hay wagon and Billy, one of our Belgian draft horses. He's strong and should be able to haul all the garbage as well as bring home a couple of dead trees for firewood."

A draft horse! Although she'd seen some of the giant animals grazing peacefully in the open fields around town, Julia had never dared approach one of them for a closer look. "That would be fine. And I'll put some extra money in your paycheck to cover the rental of your animal and wagon."

"My *vadder* is not using Billy or the wagon right now. There is no need to pay for their use," he said.

"Oh yes, there is." Cutting him off, she bent over to pick up a bucket of murky soap water she'd been using to scrub the grimy floor.

Since she didn't own a car or truck of her own, Julia was grateful for the use of Martin's horse and intended to compensate him fairly. He seemed much too generous. She really liked Martin and didn't want to take advantage of him or his resources.

When she looked up again, she found him watching her, a perplexed expression tugging at his forehead.

"How old are you?" Martin asked her suddenly.

She blinked, as though surprised by his blunt question. "That's kind of personal, don't you think?"

He looked away, thinking he shouldn't have asked. Sometimes he was as bad as Hank. His blunt candor had gotten him into trouble on more than one occasion. His mother had told him not to ask women such personal questions but he really wanted to know.

"I was just wondering," he said.

"I'm twenty-three. Why were you wondering?"

He glanced at her, his gaze moving quickly from her face to her white tennis shoes. "Don't you have a boyfriend? You're kind of old to still be single."

She pressed a hand against her chest and laughed. "Wow! I didn't think so but you obviously do. It's not as if I'm an old maid. Is it?"

He laughed, too, relieved that she wasn't angry with him. "*Ne*, you're definitely not old, but by Amish standards, you would be considered on the edge of becoming a spinster."

Her mouth dropped open and a bit of mischief sparkled in her eyes. "Really? A spinster, huh?"

Actually, by Amish standards, she already was but he couldn't think of her that way. Not this lovely, intelligent woman.

"How old are you?" she asked, turning the tables on him.

"Twenty-five. My *mudder* fears I will become a dried-up old bachelor, useful to no one."

"I doubt that. You have been a lot of use to me. Look at all the good work you've already done."

He turned away and studied the two sawhorses he'd set up on the front porch for cutting boards. "But I have no sons and no daughters to take up my work once I am old. I have no one to pass on my knowledge and my faith to."

She hesitated. "If it makes a difference, I was engaged once, but it…it didn't work out."

He caught an expression of pain in her eyes, but then it was gone so fast that he thought he must have imagined it. He nodded, wishing he'd kept his big mouth shut. It wasn't his business and he couldn't help thinking this was one of those times when his mother would have told him he was too curious and bold for an Amish man.

"I can't imagine you never marrying," she said.

He tilted his head and gazed at her with amazement. "Why do you say that?"

She shrugged one shoulder. "You seem like a family man, that's all. The way you handle yourself. The way you act with Hank. You should be married with an adoring wife and a passel of children around you."

He laughed. "I'm afraid my *mudder* and *vadder* both agree with you." He agreed, too, but what could he do? He couldn't produce a wife for himself out of thin air.

"So, why haven't you married?" she asked.

He tried to swallow, his throat suddenly dry as sandpaper. "I guess I haven't found the right girl."

"Me either. Or rather, I haven't found the right guy."

He smiled at that.

"Unfortunately, it's not quite that easy to find a suitable spouse, is it?" She glanced down, and her face flushed a pretty shade of pink.

"*Ne*, it certainly hasn't been for me."

"Frankly, I think I'm better off staying single."

He almost gasped out loud but caught himself in time. Not marry? Stay single? He could hardly contemplate such a situation. Not for himself and not for her.

"Why do you say that?" he asked.

She shrugged. "Love hurts too much. If I don't fall in love, I can't be hurt. It's that simple. I'd rather focus on my soap business and build some security for my mom and me. Then I'm in control. I get to say what happens in my life and I'm not at the whim and pleasure of someone who doesn't really care about me."

He nodded his assent. "It is true that if you don't love, you won't be hurt. But you also won't have the joy. And besides, if you marry a man who really loves you, he would never want to hurt you."

"Have you been in love before?" she asked.

"*Ne.*"

"Then how can you know for sure?"

"I sense it in here." He touched his chest, just over his heart. "When I find the right person, I will know. I'll give my whole heart to her and she'll give her whole heart to me. It will be amazing. I know it."

She was quiet for a moment, her face filled with such sadness that he thought she might cry. "I have loved before but he didn't love me in return. He used me. He abandoned me when I needed him most. It hurt more than I can say. Love isn't all it's cracked up to be, Martin. It can be brutal, cruel and destructive."

He realized what she said was true. And yet, he couldn't give up hope. Not for himself. And not for her. He just couldn't. "But it can be *wundervoll*, too."

"For you, perhaps."

"For you, as well. You must have faith. Don't give up on the Lord," he said.

Her lips trembled and he thought she was holding back the tears. "Faith is good for you and other people but it hasn't worked for me. Still, I want to have faith. I want to believe that God really cares for me."

Her words bludgeoned his heart. He hated the thought that this beautiful woman would give up on love. To him, it was the same as giving up on *Gott*.

"He does. You can believe that. You mustn't give up on finding someone to love," he said.

She looked away. "I don't know if I'm willing to try it a second time."

He didn't know what to say. He hated that someone had hurt her so badly.

"Well, I've got some soap to cut into bars," she said, clearly changing the subject.

"You made soap?"

She nodded. "Just a double batch in my kitchen last night. I want to send off some samples to commercial vendors, to see if I can get some more wholesale contracts. I also want to ensure we have enough bars to stock the store for our grand opening the first of December. So, I'd better get back to work."

"*Ja*, me, too."

He picked up a board he had already measured and marked with a pencil. With several quick movements, he cut through the wood with his handsaw. When he turned, she was gone. And just like that, his chest felt empty inside.

To take his mind off their conversation, he focused on his work. With Hank occupied upstairs with Sharon, Martin got one entire set of shelves completed before it was time to go home.

As if on cue, Julia returned and accompanied him outside. Her interest in prayer a few days earlier when he and Hank had been eating lunch had delighted him and he felt compelled to ask a question that had been weighing heavily on his mind all afternoon.

"Would you like to attend church with me tomorrow?" he asked.

Her smile dropped like a stone and she hesitated, hugging herself against the chilly wind. "I, um, I'm not sure."

"We only hold Church Sunday every other week," he hurried on before she could say no. "We hold services in our barns because they're big enough to hold the entire *Gmay*. Each *familye* in the congregation takes turns hosting the meetings. Tomorrow, church will be held at my parents' farm."

"Oh. Where do you live?" she asked.

"Three miles outside of town, along Cherry Creek."

"*Ja*, we live just off the county road," Hank interjected.

Martin whirled around as his brother joined them. He held a huge cinnamon roll that dripped with white icing. Opening wide, he took a big bite before speaking with a full mouth. "Look what Sharon gave me."

"Mrs. Rose," Martin corrected the boy.

Hank ignored his brother as he swallowed and smiled at Julia. "You want one? Your mom has lots upstairs."

"Maybe later." Julia smiled before turning back to Martin.

"If you're interested in prayer, I figure you could learn more at church," Martin said.

Though she insisted she'd given up on love, Martin wasn't so sure. Her interest in prayer meant there was a glimmer of hope inside her. But then he reconsidered.

Why had he asked? It was presumptuous and rude and much too forward of him. She was an *Englischer*, after all. His parents might not approve of him inviting her to church.

"I… I think I'd like that very much. But how will I get out there? I don't own a car," she said.

She wanted to go!

A feeling of relief and pure panic enveloped Martin at the same time. Relief because he really wanted her to come to church and panic because he knew she was an outsider and he wasn't sure how she would take it all in. It was rare for an *Englischer* to attend their church, which was spoken entirely in Pennsylvania Dutch and German. Julia wouldn't understand what was going on. Everything might seem odd to her and he didn't want to alienate her.

Hank waved a hand in the air before licking icing off his thick fingers. "We can come get you."

Martin nodded. "*Ja*, I'll pick you up in the buggy and bring you home afterward."

"And you can be my girl," Hank said.

Martin gasped, then coughed. "Hank…"

Julia's eyes widened, then she smiled. "I'm definitely your friend, Hank."

"My girlfriend?" the boy asked, looking way too eager.

Julia hesitated, seeming to choose her words carefully. "Well, I'm a girl and I'm your friend. But I'm much too old for you."

The boy's face lit up like a house on fire. "*Ach*, so you're my *maedel*."

Julia looked confused. And little wonder. She didn't speak Deitsch and had no idea that Hank had just called her his girl.

Martin bit his tongue to keep from scolding his brother. At least not now, in front of Julia.

She blinked, turning her attention back to Martin. "Isn't it a rather long distance for you to drive your horse just to pick me up for church?"

"Not at all. That's how I get here to work every day and that's what our horses are for. Your *mudder* is invited, as well," Martin said.

There. That was *gut*. If her mother accompanied them, it wouldn't seem so odd to the members of the *Gmay*. After all, he didn't want his parents or siblings to believe he was interested in Julia romantically, because he wasn't. No, not at all.

A dubious expression covered her face. "I doubt Mom would like to come but I'll invite her just in case. Are you sure you don't mind picking me up?"

"*Ne*, it would be my pleasure. But I would like to make one request."

"And what is that?"

He cleared his throat, which felt suddenly tight. "That you keep an open mind at everything you see and hear and try to feel with your heart. Try not to make any judgments until I can clarify things for you."

As Martin explained about the language barrier and that she might not understand everything that went on at church, Hank continued to stare at Julia with open adoration.

"Don't worry if there is something you can't understand. Things may seem odd at first but we have a reason for everything we do. I promise to expand on it afterward, during the ride when I bring you home. I'll answer all your questions then," Martin said.

She smiled happily. "Of course. We'll have a long chat. Thank you. I'd like to join you very much."

Martin exhaled a slow breath, hoping his invitation wasn't a mistake. It was too late to take back his offer now. Instead, he told her what time he would need to collect her so they wouldn't be late for services.

"I'll be ready," she said.

He nodded, then loaded his toolbox in the back of his wagon. While he herded Hank into the buggy, Julia didn't leave the front porch. She stood watching them with a thoughtful expression tugging at her forehead. As he drove out of the parking lot, she waved and a feeling of absolute dread swept over Martin.

Now he'd done it. He'd only recently met Julia, yet he wanted nothing more than to teach her about his faith. To help her understand his beliefs and perhaps discover her own relationship with *Gott*. Faith was such a huge part of Martin's life. It governed everything he did and he loved it dearly, but his people didn't actively proselytize. They never saw the need to share their religion with outsiders and preferred to show their beliefs in their daily living. So what would Bishop Yoder say when he discovered

Martin had invited an unmarried *Englisch* woman and her mother to church? Worse yet, what would Martin's parents say? As an older unmarried man, he was already fodder for the gossips in his *Gmay*. The last thing he needed was to be associated with an *Englisch* woman.

Yet he couldn't help it. He felt compelled to invite her. And he couldn't take the invitation back. Not now that she had accepted. He'd just have to move forward and hope for the best.

Chapter Five

"You're not serious."

Sharon Rose stared at her daughter with absolute astonishment. Sitting at the dinner table that evening, Julia set her spoon on the table, her stew growing cold in the bowl. She had just told her mom about Martin's invitation to attend church in the morning. But she hated the look of frosty abhorrence in her mother's eyes. Maybe it had been a mistake to tell her. Maybe she should back out.

"I'm very serious, Mom. We've both been invited."

Mom gave a caustic laugh as she reached for a freshly baked roll, squishing it in her grasp. "Well, I sure won't be attending. Not in a million years." She threw a glance at Julia. "I thought you were going to make another batch of soap to cure before our grand opening."

"I've made a number of single batches almost every evening since we arrived in Colorado and they're curing nicely. It won't hurt to take time off to worship God. Don't worry. We'll have enough soap for our grand opening and to mail off to vendors, too."

"You're not really planning to attend the Amish church, are you?" Mom asked.

Julia reached for her glass and took a sip of warm milk before answering slowly. "Yes, I am."

Mom's lips tightened. "It's that young man, isn't it? Martin. You find him attractive."

It was a statement, not a question.

"Martin is just our handyman, nothing more. You didn't mind the two times when I went to Bible study with Debbie. Dallin went with us, too."

She had listened to a couple of people pray at these meetings but had never done so herself.

"That was different," Mom said.

"How so?"

"Debbie wasn't Amish. Neither was Dallin."

Julia placed her elbow on the table and leaned forward, feeling confused. "No, but they were both dishonest. So, is it just the Amish church you object to? Or Martin?"

"Both, I'm afraid. They are one and the same. If you go with that young man, he'll…he'll…"

"He'll what, Mom? Why don't you like him?"

Mom pushed her bowl away, obviously having lost her appetite. "I don't dislike him. But you're too free-thinking to be Amish. You have a mind of your own and shouldn't have to suppress that. And honestly, I'm afraid he'll corrupt your ideas. The Amish aren't like normal people."

Julia laughed. "That's a compliment, Mom. And what are normal people like? I'm not sure I've ever met one."

Mom frowned. "Amish men dominate their women. They rule their homes with an iron fist."

Julia was aghast. Her father had been such a kind,

gentle man. She couldn't imagine being married to a dominating brute. "How do you know what Amish men are like?"

"I... I've heard things over the years. I knew some Amish women once, before you were born."

"You like Hank well enough. He comes upstairs and you feed him all the time," Julia said.

"He's no threat to us. He's just a boy with Down syndrome and he deserves a little kindness," Mom said.

"But you don't seem to like Martin at all."

"He's a fully grown man and he doesn't have Down syndrome," Mom said.

Her justification seemed a bit off to Julia and she released a sigh. "I'm just going to church with him. It's not as if I'm going to become Amish. It's just this one time."

Her mother continued to gaze at her and Julia felt compelled to explain.

"I asked him some questions about his faith and he's the first person to give me straight answers that I liked. I don't know why you disapprove so much."

"Because he's Amish, dear. Amish. They don't even use electricity," Mom said.

Julia snorted as she scooted her chair back from the table. "Well, neither do we."

She glanced at the freshly painted ceiling where a light fixture was attached. Because they had no power, the bulbs were dead and they were still using kerosene lamps to light their way.

"That will change once we can pay to have an electrician repair our power problem. When do you think we'll be able to afford that?" Mom asked.

No longer feeling hungry, Julia set her bowl in the sink and filled it with hot soapy water. "It could be a little while. We'll have to see how the grand opening goes. I want to ensure we have enough money to pay our bills first. Since we've lived without electricity even before we moved to Colorado, I thought we could wait a little longer and save some money."

"Yes, we can wait," Mom conceded.

"And I'm going to church tomorrow. It's just one time and it'll probably come to nothing. But I'd really like to go."

Mom released a deep sigh. "Suit yourself."

What else could Sharon say? Julia was a grown woman. But they didn't speak while Julia washed and Mom dried the dishes. Julia could feel the tension in the air like a living, breathing thing. She hated having friction with her mother. Again, she thought about backing out and not going but had no idea how to get word to Martin so he wouldn't drive all the way into town to pick her up early in the morning. Once he arrived, it wouldn't be fair to tell him he'd come all this way for nothing. Right?

"I'm tired and going to bed now. Remember that I love you more than anything else in the world." Mom leaned close and kissed her cheek.

"I know. I love you, too, Mom." Julia spoke quietly, not knowing what else to say.

She watched as Mom picked up a lamp and carried it to her bedroom. She limped slightly, indicating that her hips were hurting her. The apartment was small but warm and cozy and Julia felt safe and happy here. She didn't want trouble with her mother.

Surely this wasn't worth arguing over. She'd go to church with Martin this one time and that would probably be the end of it. No more questions. No more curiosity about God. That would please her mother. Surely everything would return to normal. She hoped.

The following morning, it was still dark when Martin pulled his horse into the parking lot at Rose Soapworks. A single light gleamed from inside the store. Taking a deep inhale of crisp air, he stepped out of the buggy. As he walked toward the front door, he could see puffs of his breath and knew the first snowfall of the season would hit any day now.

There was no need to knock. Julia must have been watching from inside because she stepped out onto the porch and met him at the bottom step.

"Good morning, Martin," she said softly, her eyes bright, her pale skin glowing in the shadows.

"*Guder mariye*, Julia," he returned.

"*Guder mariye,*" she repeated with perfect pronunciation.

He smiled as she laid a gloved hand on his arm and he accompanied her to the buggy. She wore a long, wool coat, her plain gray scarf tucked high around her neck. Though he could see her ankles and knew she must be wearing a dress, her low-heeled black shoes were quite simple by *Englisch* standards. She'd pulled her long hair back in a tidy bun at the nape of her neck and wore no makeup that he could see. For an *Englisch* woman, she dressed quite plain, but he knew his mother would not approve of the large gold buttons on her coat.

As he helped her into the buggy, he was highly aware of the energy pulsing between them. "Is your *mudder* not coming with us?"

Julia shook her head. "No, she's not happy about me going either."

He glanced at the dark building. "I'm sorry. I don't want to create conflict between you and your *mudder*. It's important to honor your *eldre* in all things."

"Eldre?" she asked.

"Your parents."

She repeated the word several times, as if trying it out on her tongue. "My *mudder* would rather I not go but she knows I'm a grown woman who can make her own choices."

He jerked, pleasantly surprised that she had used a Deitsch word in her vocabulary. But contention was not of *Gott* and honoring parents was highly important to all Amish people.

"Where's Hank?" she asked as she settled herself on the cold front seat.

He reached for a quilt his *familye* kept in the back for traveling during the winter months. "He's at home, helping set up for church." Martin spread the quilt across her legs.

"Danke," she said, sliding her hands beneath the heavy fabric and pulling it up to her waist.

Again, he was surprised. "You're speaking Deitsch now?"

She shrugged, a light smile teasing the corners of her lips. "It seems appropriate. Maybe you can teach me your language."

Ah, he liked that, but he couldn't explain why. She was so different from most *Englischers* he'd met. So humble and eager to learn and try new things. "You don't think your *mudder* would mind?"

"Ne, I can handle my *mudder*," she said.

Again, he smiled, inordinately pleased by her efforts

to speak his language. Taking the lead lines into his hands, he slapped them lightly against the horse's back.

"Schritt!" he called.

The horse stepped forward.

"I'll bet Hank wasn't happy to be left behind today," Julia said.

Martin smiled, remembering the temper tantrum his younger brother had thrown when he'd been told he couldn't ride into town to pick up Julia. *"Ne,* he was not happy about it at all."

Neither would his mother be pleased when she found out that Sharon wasn't accompanying them. The only reason his father had agreed to let Martin pick up Julia alone was because he thought they'd be chaperoned by her mother. But there was no help for it now.

"Is Hank your only sibling?" Julia asked.

"Ne, I have three sisters and another brother. I am the eldest."

Her eyes widened and she stared at the road. "Wow! That's six children! Your mother, er, *mudder* must have her hands full."

He chuckled at her comment. "Do you think that's a lot?"

"It sure is. Most people only want one or two kids these days. Or none at all."

"Not us. Children are precious to my people. The average Amish *familye* has six or seven *kinder.* We want all the *gut* Lord will send us. We believe *kinder* are a gift from *Gott."*

"That's a nice way to look at it. But isn't that a lot of extra mouths to feed?" she asked.

He shrugged. *"Ja,* but they also make many hands to work on the farm. And as they marry, our *familye* expands and we have many people we can call on whenever we need help during times of trouble."

She smiled. "Many hands make light work, or so my *mudder* always says."

He nodded. "Exactly. I have a large *familye* I can depend upon. I'll never be alone no matter what."

She was quiet for several moments, as if thinking this over. "It would have been nice when my *vadder* was ill to have *familye* members to depend on. But I was on my own. It's been difficult being an only *kinder.*"

"Kind," he corrected. "Two children are *kinder*, but one child is *kind.*"

She smiled at his explanation and doggedly repeated the words. "I always wanted a brother or sister, or both. My *mudder* just wasn't able to have any more after I was born."

"If your parents wanted more, I'm sorry to hear they couldn't."

"My mom told me she almost died giving birth to me."

Martin grunted in acknowledgement. "It happens that way sometimes."

"What is the word for brother and sister?" she asked.

He gave her the words and waited as she repeated them several times.

"Do you really want to learn Deitsch?" he asked.

She hesitated. *"Ja*, I think I'd like that very much. It could be useful when the Amish come into my new store to do business."

He smiled, unable to contain his delight. "Then I'll do my best to teach you."

They rode in silence for several minutes, enjoying the view of the sun peeking over the tops of the eastern mountains. Fingers of pink, gold and purple painted the valley below. A cluster of black-and-white cows stood grazing in a fallow field, the nubs of dried grass glistening with a layer of early morning frost.

"It's so beautiful here," Julia said.

Martin looked at her, seeing the peaceful contentment on her face. "*Ja*, it sure is."

"Why is marriage so important to your people?" she asked.

He looked away, embarrassed to be caught staring. "*Ach*, because *familye* is so important to us. Without marriage, there is no *familye* and no *kinder* and our way of life would die. Do you…do you want children one day?"

Oh, maybe he shouldn't have asked that. It might sound too presumptuous.

A soft smile curved her lips. "*Ja*, someday if I ever get married."

"Do you…do you want lots of *kinder*, or only one or two?"

"I think I'd like more, but that's a long way off."

He nodded, accepting this. After all, he could never be her husband so it really didn't concern him.

"I may never marry," she said.

He snorted. "Of course you will. Everyone weds. Don't they?"

After all, he still wasn't married. But the thought that he might remain a bachelor all his life had never taken hold in his mind. He hadn't found a suitable wife yet but he knew deep in his heart that he would one day. He'd always had faith that *Gott* hadn't abandoned him. But lately, he wasn't so sure.

"Many people choose not to marry. Or they postpone marriage for a long time. They choose a career instead," she said.

He blinked, staring straight ahead at the black asphalt. "Why can't they have both?"

She shrugged. "I guess they could."

"I want a large *familye*. When I die, I doubt I'll be concerned that I didn't earn enough money. I'll be concerned with how I treated my *familye* and whether I spent enough time with them. That is what really matters. Your *familye* is all you get to take with you in the end."

She looked down at her hands folded primly in her lap. He hoped he hadn't said anything to upset her. After all, he was laying quite a bit of new information on her and it could be rather overwhelming.

"I can't imagine living my life alone either but sometimes we don't get a choice in the matter." She spoke so softly that he almost didn't hear.

Her words sounded so lonely, so hollow, that he felt a rush of empathy for her. And then he knew that neither of them wanted to be alone. Neither of them had chosen not to marry but the opportunity to marry someone who could make them happy had never come their way. Yet.

For the first time in a very long time, Martin wondered if he might remain a solitary bachelor after all.

Chapter Six

The rhythmic clip-clop of the horse's hooves on the pavement seemed so relaxing to Julia. Still, a feeling of anticipation buzzed through her. This was her first buggy ride and her first time attending an Amish church meeting. Everything about Martin seemed new and interesting. It had been a long time since she'd enjoyed a fun outing with friends. But this was so much more. Finally, she could explore the feelings she had for God. Her relationship with God had been pretty lean up to this point and she was hungry to learn more about the Lord.

"Are you nervous?" Martin asked, giving a quick flick of the lead lines to keep the horse going at a steady pace.

"A little," she confessed.

"Don't be. Everything will be fine."

He then described what she should expect. How the church meeting would culminate with lunch afterward. Of course, she had a zillion questions but he answered every one. Their animated discussion brought her a sense of exhilaration. It tantalized her intellect and made her immensely happy. Martin's calm voice sounded so reasonable. It made her feel as if she'd known him all her life. He demystified God and made her feel closer to her Heavenly Father.

Though the day was crisp, the bright sun glimmered in the eastern sky. As they pulled into the yard of his family's farm along Cherry Creek, Julia gazed at the wide pastures surrounding the two-story log house and enormous red barn.

Martin pointed at several black-and-white cows standing in a pasture at the side of the barn. "Those are our milk cows."

Julia blinked, feeling as if she'd stepped back in time to a quaint, bygone era of wholesome living.

Fields of hay lay fallow with brown stubble from the autumn harvest. The barbed wire fences were straight and orderly, the flower beds bordering the house cleared of frozen flowers and weed free. Not surprising. She'd already learned that Martin was hardworking and fastidious. No doubt his parents had taught him well.

The place seemed deserted. No one was there to greet them.

"Schtopp!" Martin called, pulling the buggy to a halt.

They paused next to a long row of black buggies parked along the outer fence. A plethora of horses grazed peacefully in the pasture next to them.

"You have so many horses," she said.

"They aren't ours. Those are the road horses everyone uses to pull their buggies. I'll put our horse in with them and then we can join the meeting," Martin said.

He hopped out and came around to assist her. The feel of his strong hand supporting her arm as she stepped down caused a warm sensation to cascade over her. She quickly straightened her skirt and patted her hair, hoping she looked all right.

"You look fine," he said, as if reading her thoughts.

She realized that was huge praise coming from this man. She'd already learned the Amish weren't given to frivolous compliments and his words pleased her enormously.

She caught the low thrum of voices lifting through the air in song. She turned toward the barn, a feeling of curiosity pulsing over her. The singing continued in long-drawn-out a capella unison. Male voices mingled with female in a solemn hymn that reminded Julia of a medieval movie she'd seen once. The sound was eerie yet beautiful.

"They have started. We must hurry." Martin spoke low.

She caught his urgency as he quickly unhitched the horse from its harness. They must be late.

"Komm." He turned and beckoned gently to her.

Julia followed as he hurried toward the barn. An older man with a full gray beard and no moustache stood at the entrance. He wore a black frock coat and felt hat. His dark, penetrating gaze shifted briefly to her and she felt his curiosity.

Her sense of ease immediately shifted to absolute panic. What was she doing here? These people were strangers. Perhaps her mother had been right and she wouldn't be welcomed. Oh, why had she come?

"It's all right." As if sensing her unease, Martin spoke softly beside her. His soothing voice helped settle her nerves.

"Julia, this is my *vadder*, David Hostetler." Martin

made the introduction in a low whisper that wouldn't disturb the singing.

"Hallo," she greeted the man softly, holding out her hand. He took it and squeezed gently, his gray eyes crinkling with a warm smile.

"Willkomm to our home," he said. Then, he faced Martin. *"Du bischt schpot!"*

Julia caught the mild tone of impatience in David's voice but no anger.

"Ja, I know we're late. I'm sorry," Martin whispered.

"Where is her *mudder*?" David asked, peering behind them.

"Mrs. Rose chose not to *komm* with us today," Martin explained.

With a brief nod, David lifted a hand to indicate they should enter the barn. A matronly woman stood just inside, as if waiting for them.

"Julia, this is my *mudder*, Linda Hostetler." Again Martin spoke low.

Julia met the woman's formal gaze. Her white prayer *kapp* stood out in sharp contrast to her simple black dress, tights and shoes. She wore a crisp, white apron over her dress that Julia found quite lovely.

"Komm and join us," Linda whispered, indicating that Julia should follow her.

The spacious interior of the barn had been swept to an immaculate cleanliness. Looking up, Julia saw rows of hard backless benches lined up where numerous worshippers sat. As she passed, Julia felt the people's eyes on her. A few smiled but some frowned. Whether they disapproved because they were late for the meeting or because she was *Englisch*, Julia wasn't sure.

Rather than sitting with their families, the assembly

was seated by gender and age with all the men and boys
on one side of the room and all the women and girls on
the other. Martin had already explained that this segre-
gation had nothing to do with discrimination but rather
symbolized accountability to the authority of the church.

Linda perched on a front bench, indicating that Julia
should join her. Julia did so, clasping her hands tightly
in her lap. Martin joined his father opposite her. Sitting
next to his father, Hank made a sound of exuberance and
lifted a hand to wave hello. Martin's father scowled and
shook his head and the boy settled down.

David and Martin immediately joined in the song
but Julia didn't know the words. Linda handed her a
hymnal titled *Ausbund* but it didn't help much since the
words were in German. Their voices united in a labori-
ous tempo without musical accompaniment.

Glancing about, Julia noticed many gazes resting
on her. Some looks were open and curious but others
were downright hostile. When she met their eyes, people
looked away, as though embarrassed to be caught gawk-
ing. Julia felt suddenly awkward. Even though she wore
modest clothes and her long hair was tied back in a bun,
the brightly flowered print of her skirt seemed garish
and out of place in comparison to the sedate solid colors
and prayer *kapps* of the Amish women.

Remembering Martin's request from the day before,
she was determined to keep an open mind and try to
feel with her heart. She glanced his way, feeling rather
anxious. And that's when he did something that immediately put her at ease.

He smiled and winked.

"Ahem!"

Martin's father cleared his throat and Julia looked

away, reminding herself to be reverent. This was church, after all. A place to worship God. She hummed along with the song. The slow tempo made it easy enough to follow. It went on and on but seemed rather sweet and she found that she enjoyed the worshipful feeling in the room. For this period of time, she pushed aside all her worldly cares and relaxed, focusing on God.

Hearing her humming, Linda tilted her head slightly and smiled with approval.

Finally, the singing ended and the preaching began. The words were spoken in Deitsch and Julia understood nothing at all. But as she gazed at the minister's intense expression and heard the loving emotion vibrating in his voice, a feeling of peace settled over Julia and she felt the devout message deep in her heart. She was certain Martin would explain the topic on their way home.

The moment church ended, Julia was surrounded by people.

"Julia!"

She whirled around and found herself engulfed in a solid hug by Hank.

"Oof!" She tried to disengage herself. "*Hallo*, Hank."

"Wie bischt du?" the boy greeted her rather loudly.

"Hank, that's enough. Remember your manners." Martin tugged his brother's arms free from Julia.

"But Julia's my girl," the boy exclaimed, drawing a number of surprised gasps.

"That's nonsense." Linda's eyes widened with disapproval.

Martin snorted. "She's just your friend. Remember? But you must not hug her. It isn't proper."

Linda breathed a sigh of relief and nodded at her son.

"But I want…" Hank began.

Martin turned away, ignoring the boy. He quickly introduced Julia to Bishop Amos Yoder, Deacon Darrin Albrecht and Minister Jeremiah Beiler, their only minister. The three men gazed at her with cautious smiles that didn't quite meet their eyes. She sensed their hesitation.

"Your *mudder* did not *komm* with you today?" Bishop Yoder asked politely.

Julia blinked, surprised that he'd known her mom might be here. She shook her head. "I'm sorry, but she isn't feeling well and chose to stay at home."

"Martin has told us she has lupus. I hope it isn't serious," the bishop said.

She didn't explain that lupus was very serious. "She'll be fine after she rests awhile."

"Perhaps she'll *komm* with you next time," Linda suggested.

"You must tell her that she is *willkomm* to join us anytime." The bishop lifted his bushy eyebrows in expectation, his bearded face showing nothing but friendship. And in that moment, Julia saw nothing to fear in his kind, intelligent eyes. She decided then that she liked Martin's parents and the church elders.

"*Ja*, perhaps," Julia said.

"I noticed you are speaking some Deitsch." David's voice was filled with approval.

Julia shrugged, feeling a bit shy. "A little bit but I fear I mispronounce most of the words."

"Already, she is learning quite fast," Martin said.

"I'm gonna help teach her, too," Hank blurted, looking mightily pleased with himself.

"*Ach*, that is *gut*. Soon, you will be able to understand what is being said during the preachings," Jeremiah Beiler exclaimed.

"*Ja*, that is very *gut*." Linda smiled, too, her expression one of relief.

They all beamed at her and Julia thought it must be because they thought she was serious about becoming Amish. The fact that Martin was unmarried and had brought her here today must worry them. She was *Englisch*, after all. A woman of the world. No doubt they preferred her to learn Deitsch and join their Amish community rather than pull Martin out of his faith.

But the fact was, she and Martin were just friends. She was here as a one-time guest and had no intention of joining the Amish faith. Especially since her mother didn't approve.

Linda glanced at the door and lifted both her hands in the air. "*Ach*, I'm the hostess today and here I stand around visiting. I should be in the kitchen helping with the meal. Would you like to join me?"

Julia met the woman's gaze, eager for the distraction. "Of course. I'd love to."

As they turned and headed toward the house, Julia changed her mind when Martin didn't move from his place beside his father. She realized he wasn't coming. Perhaps meals were considered a woman's chore and he was expected to remain with the men. Because she wanted to be polite, she followed Linda.

They crossed the green lawn and Julia noticed numerous long tables set up in the backyard. Sitting beneath the branches of a tall elm tree, a rather elderly lady spoke in a loud whisper that wasn't really a whisper at all and carried clear across the yard.

"If you ask me, Martin has become so desperate for a wife that he's now looking at the *Englisch* girls," the elderly woman said. "You mark my words. Martin will be pulled out of our faith if something isn't done to stop it."

"Marva, what are you saying?" a middle-aged woman asked with incredulous wonder.

"Just that we might lose him," Marva said, lifting her head in an imperious gesture.

Linda came to a halt, staring at the two women as her face contorted with fear and disapproval.

Seeing Linda's expression, the middle-aged woman hurried to alleviate the situation. "*Ach*, Martin would never abandon his faith. He's steadfast. That's why he brought the girl here. Surely she'll convert."

"And what if she doesn't?" Marva asked, her lips pursed like a prune. Looking straight at Linda, she seemed to challenge her, not caring at all that Julia was listening to their words.

"Idle gossip is an unworthy endeavor," Linda said before turning toward the house.

Marva released a pensive "harrumph."

Julia followed after Linda but heard Marva's parting comment.

"The girl seems vaguely familiar to me, though I can't remember how. I feel as if I know her from somewhere," Marva said.

"You probably saw her in town once," the younger woman said.

"*Ne*, I don't think so. I feel certain that I know her from my life back in Ohio, though I don't see how since she's so young and it's been many years since I lived there."

Julia slipped inside behind Linda. As the screen door clapped closed behind her, she breathed a sigh of relief. Maybe she didn't belong here after all.

Linda paused in the laundry room, resting a hand against her heart, taking deep inhales.

"Are you all right?" Julia asked.

"*Ja*, I'm sorry you had to hear that. Please ignore what they said. Marva Geingerich is a *Swartzentruber* and doesn't approve of anyone," Linda explained.

"A *Swartzentruber*?"

"*Ja*, the *Swartzentrubers* are Old Order Amish and shun any and all change. Marva just turned eighty-nine and thinks she knows everything. I don't happen to share her opinions. Now, *komm* and slice some bread."

Through the open doorway into the kitchen, Julia saw numerous women milling around the counters in organized chaos as they prepared the noon meal. The buzz of their voices mingled together in happy banter. Their dresses were identical with a myriad of solid dark colors, white aprons and *kapps*. She watched in fascination, stunned by the enormous amount of food they had placed on a trestle table.

Without another word, Linda hurried over to the table and handed Julia a loaf of homemade bread and a knife. The women greeted them.

As they worked, Linda made introductions. Naomi Fisher, who looked to be about sixty-five years of age. Lori Geingerich and her four-year-old daughter, Rachel. Lizzie Stoltzfus and Abby Fisher, who were both newly-weds and appeared to be about Julia's age. Sarah Yoder, the bishop's wife. And several other older women. They were all friendly and smiled in welcome.

"I'll try to remember all your names." Julia gave a little laugh as she slid the sharp knife through the loaf of bread.

"Don't worry. You'll soon know all of us quite well and we'll be *gut* friends." Abby spoke in a buoyant voice.

Lizzie looked up from where she was slicing red apples beside the sink. "Martin tells us that you're opening a soap studio in town."

Everyone turned to look at her and Julia's guard went up like a kite flying high.

"*Ja*, that is why I want to learn Deitsch. So I can speak with all of you when you come in to my new store," Julia replied.

There. That was good, wasn't it? An open invitation to visit and be friends.

Sarah Yoder laughed out loud. Not a sarcastic laugh but simply one of good humor. "That's nice, but I'm afraid we all make our own soap. We really don't have a reason to buy it elsewhere. In fact, Lizzie sells soaps, too."

Oh. Maybe her attempt to find common ground hadn't worked after all. She hadn't expected to be in commercial conflict with any of them.

"Um, perhaps you'd like to sell some of your soaps on consignment in my store," she offered.

Lizzie nodded. "Perhaps."

"May I ask what fragrances you use in your soap making?" Julia asked.

Naomi waved a dismissive hand before returning to the pot of soup she was stirring. "We don't use fragrance. That would be too worldly for our needs."

"But Julia sells her soaps to the *Englisch*, don't you? So I'm sure you use fragrance. That's what appeals to your *Englisch* customers. We do the same when we make things to sell to the *Englisch*, but we don't use it in our own homes." Sarah spoke in a kind tone.

Julia smiled, trying not to show her anxiety. She gazed at the beautiful rag rug beneath her feet, thinking it would take time to get used to these people and their ways. "Yes, that's true. I sell my soaps to anyone who will buy them."

"*Ach*, I don't know any self-respecting Amish woman who would buy soap when she can make it herself," Naomi said. Again, there was no cruelty in her statement but just a simple truth.

A flush of embarrassed heat suffused Julia's face. She was quickly learning how self-sufficient the Amish were. "I... I'm sure all of you are great soap makers. Perhaps you might teach me some of your methods."

"That sounds fun. And maybe you can teach us some of your techniques," Abby said, smiling sweetly.

"Absolutely. And I love the color of your dress. Did you make it?" Julia eyed the lovely dark rose color, thinking all of their dresses were beautiful in their simplicity.

"*Ja*, we make all our clothes," Abby said.

At that moment, Marva Geingerich, the old *Swartzentruber* woman, came into the room. The thud of her cane pounded the bare floor with each step. With her presence, Julia's hands felt trembly.

"If you become Amish, you'll have to learn to sew." Marva spoke the words in a stern, warning voice.

Linda lifted her head. "*Ach*, there's nothing to sewing. I'll teach you. If you can make soap, you can certainly learn to sew."

Julia wasn't sure she wanted to learn. Nor did she plan to join the Amish but she didn't say so. Instead, she changed the subject.

"This rag rug is beautiful. Did you make it?" she asked Linda.

"*Ja*, I used all the leftover scraps of cloth I've collected over the years."

"Maybe you would like to sell your rugs in my store on consignment, too," Julia suggested.

Linda paused as she filled a teapot full of boiling hot water. Then, she smiled wide. "*Ja*, I would like that. That's very generous of you."

Julia shrugged. "The way I look at it, any kind of business can be good for all of us."

Several women stopped their various chores to look quizzically at her, but Julia just ducked her head and kept slicing. She realized then that making soap was simply part of Amish life. Rather than finding common ground with these women, Julia sensed that she had offended them and she wasn't sure how to make things right. Perhaps it would be best to shut her mouth, get through the meal and hope that Martin took her home soon. Except for sitting on a hard bench all morning, she'd done nothing today. No real physical labor. But it didn't seem to matter. She was absolutely exhausted and ready to leave.

"Martin, I see you've brought an *Englischer* to church with you today."

Martin turned and saw Ezekiel Burkholder gazing at him intently from where he sat at the table waiting for his noon meal. At the age of ninety-five, *Dawdi* Zeke, as they called him, was the eldest member of their *Gmay*. With sparkling gray eyes and shocking white hair and beard, the man was still spry and in complete control of his mental faculties.

Martin walked over to the old patriarch and sat down

opposite him. "*Ja*, she is an *Englischer*. Her name is Julia Rose."

Several men, including Martin's father, Bishop Yoder and Deacon Albrecht, sat nearby and Martin realized he was about to get a grilling from them. Before he left this evening, Martin had no doubt they all would know everything they possibly could about Julia and her family. He couldn't help wondering if she was facing the same dilemma inside the kitchen. What was taking her so long? She'd gone inside the house with his mother some time ago and he was anxious to know how she was doing.

"How did you meet this woman?" *Dawdi* Zeke asked.

Martin explained about his job at Rose Soapworks.

"It's *gut* that you are earning money to pay for your barn. But what are your intentions with this woman?"

Here it was. The question Martin had known would come up eventually. A question he wished to avoid.

"I have no intentions at all. She is just a friend and my employer. She expressed an interest in my faith so I brought her to church. I also invited her *mudder* but she didn't want to *komm*," he said.

"He is even teaching Julia to speak Deitsch," David said. His comment was accompanied by a round of *ahhs* and approving nods.

"The best marriages start with a man and woman becoming *gut* friends," *Dawdi* Zeke said.

Several men nodded again, including David, who sat back in his seat, his gaze narrowed on his son. Martin could feel their intensity. Unless Julia converted to their faith, becoming friends with the *Englischer* could only lead to trouble. Especially for an unmarried Amish man in desperate need of a wife.

"When I marry, I will wed an Amish woman or not at all," Martin reassured them, noticing that his father's tensed shoulders relaxed a bit. "But Julia has expressed a great interest in our faith, so I felt it was my duty to lead her to the Lord."

There, that was good. It was the truth, after all. Martin knew that none of the men could argue with this logic. Though they didn't actively proselytize, they still had an obligation to teach the truth when someone asked them for the information.

"That is *gut*, as long as you are vigilant and careful not to be swayed to accept the worldly values the *Englisch* seem to cherish," Bishop Yoder said.

"*Ja*, you must be wary lest this woman tries to entice you to an *Englisch* life," Deacon Albrecht added.

Martin soon found himself receiving all sorts of advice on how to stay strong in his faith while leading Julia to the truth. Having anticipated this beforehand, he took it all in stride.

But as he listened, his thoughts turned to Julia. When they'd first arrived late to the meeting, he could see that she didn't want to be here. He could see the panic written all across her face. Her eyes had widened with amazement, her forehead crinkled in confusion. What seemed normal and mundane to him must seem so strange and eccentric to her.

Then, the minister had started to speak. Julia's attention had been rapt on the man. As she listened, a look of peace had covered her glowing face. She looked so innocent and pure sitting there in his father's barn. He'd felt highly attracted to her. But just one problem: she wasn't Amish.

To love and marry outside his faith, he would be

shunned by his people. They wouldn't speak to him nor take anything from his hand. He couldn't do business with them. He couldn't do anything. For those reasons, he would never do anything to get himself shunned, no matter how much he longed for a wife and *familye* of his own.

At that moment, a stream of women came from the house carrying a variety of bowls and platters of food. The moment he saw the flash of Julia's bright skirt, his senses went on high alert. Not wanting to appear too eager, he forced himself to drag his gaze away as she carried a tea service over to *Dawdi* Zeke and set it on the table. Little four-year-old Rachel Geingerich followed with a plate of cookies for the elderly man. The girl stumbled across the uneven grass, almost dropping her cargo before Julia rescued her.

"Here, let me help you." She spoke kindly to the child as she took her arm while the girl regained her footing.

"Danke," Rachel said, her voice high and sweet as she set the plate on the table next to Zeke.

"I will be going into the mountains in a few days, to collect some firewood," Martin said. Speaking in Deitsch, he'd purposefully changed the subject. If his father wasn't interested in helping gather the wood, he didn't want Julia to know.

David tilted his head. "Why do you need firewood? It's late in the season and we have plenty here for our needs."

"It's for Julia and her *mudder*. They have recently arrived in Riverton and will need fuel for their wood-burning stoves. I thought I could go get some before the snow flies."

"*Ach*, it sounds like it's time for a frolic." Bishop Yoder slapped his hands against his thighs and smiled wide.

"I can help," Jakob Fisher offered.

"And me also," Will Lapp said.

"*Ja*, we can get a work party together and take care of the chore in one trip. We might need an additional day to cut the wood into smaller pieces but that shouldn't be too difficult," the bishop suggested.

Martin nodded, eager for their help. A frolic was usually work-based, with men and women helping to accomplish a specific task. It was a time for catching up on one another's business while they worked to bless someone else's life. And it always included a nice meal at the end. He had wondered how he would have time to bring in enough fuel for Julia's needs before the first snowfall.

Within a few minutes, the frolic was organized and he couldn't help feeling overwhelmed by the willingness of his *Gmay* to pitch in. It was one of the reasons he loved his faith so much. Service was an integral part of the Amish religion and he was overjoyed to be a part of it.

"Rachel! Look out!"

Martin whipped around and saw little Rachel reaching for the teapot filled with scalding hot water. As if in slow motion, he saw the child standing on tiptoe to grasp the handle of the teapot with her tiny hands. Sitting in front of her was a cup and saucer. No doubt she intended to pour a cup of tea for *Dawdi* Zeke. But the pot tilted, the lid slid off and the steam rose from the opening as hot water sloshed over the rim.

Seeing the danger, Martin tried to react, but he wasn't quick enough. Instead, Julia knocked the pot askew. It tipped over but, instead of dousing Rachel's head with boiling water, it washed over Julia's left hand and wrist.

"Ouch!" Julia cried. She shook the hot water off, then held her hand close to her chest to ease the pain.

Before Martin could take another breath, he saw her skin turn a bright, angry red. Tears filled her eyes and he shot out of his seat.

"*Mamm!* We need cold water now," he yelled.

Out of the corner of his eye, he saw his mother turn, see the dilemma and send a boy sprinting to the spring house. Linda grabbed a pitcher of chilled water from off one of the tables and hurried over to Julia.

"Put your hand in here. There, my *liebchen*," she cooed as she thrust Julia's entire hand and wrist into the cooling liquid.

"Eli! We need Eli now!" Martin searched the congregation for the man.

Eli Stoltzfus stood up from his place at the opposite end of the yard and came running. "What is it?"

"She is badly burned," Martin said.

While Martin got Julia a chair to sit on, Eli inspected her injuries. Tears freely ran down her face and she bit her bottom lip. Martin thought she was doing an admirable job of trying not to cry. It took everything within him not to cry, too. How he wished he could take her pain upon himself. He hated to see her injured.

"You have a bad scald," Eli told her.

"Are you a doctor?" Julia asked, her voice vibrating. She looked pale and frightened.

"*Ne*, but I am a certified paramedic."

The boy returned with a bucket of water from the spring house. Eli submerged her hand in the fresh, chilled liquid.

"I… I didn't know the Amish could be paramedics."

Surprise flashed in Julia's eyes. She looked so incredulous that several people around her chuckled.

"You'd be surprised what we can be," Eli spoke without looking up.

The paramedic studied her skin. Martin was stunned to see huge blisters forming right before his eyes. They covered the top of her hand and fingers and extended up her wrist.

The commotion had brought the attention of almost the entire congregation. Hank crowded close to see what was amiss.

"Julia! Are you all right?" the boy asked, his eyes wide with anxiety as he pushed his spectacles up the bridge of his nose. Always kind and loving, he rubbed her shoulder in a circular motion.

At that moment, Julia appeared to be gritting her teeth. She nodded and showed a weak smile to the boy. "Don't worry, Hank. I'm all right."

But she wasn't. Martin could tell by looking at her wan face and the angry red burns. The fact that she would offer comfort to Hank when she was in distress caused Martin's respect for her to grow. She wasn't a weak or silly woman. She was strong and compassionate and filled with faith.

If only she were Amish.

"*Ach*, you poor dear," Naomi said.

"She saved my Rachel. Did you see? If she hadn't knocked the pot aside, it would have spilled boiling water all over my little girl." Lori Geingerich spoke with disbelief as she hugged Rachel to her chest.

"*Mamm*, is Julia gonna be okay?" Rachel asked, her voice quivering with tears.

Linda answered instead. "Of course she is. We're going to take *gut* care of her."

She also rested a comforting hand on Julia's back. Seeing his mother's compassion for this *Englisch* woman caused a hard lump to form in Martin's throat. How he loved his *familye*. How he loved his faith. It didn't matter right now that Julia was an outsider. In this moment, they would care for her like they would one of their own.

"We could put butter on the burns," Sarah kindly suggested.

"*Ne*, Eli says that's the worst thing we can do for a burn since it holds the heat into the wound. Cooling compresses are best," Lizzie said.

"*Ach*, I'm glad to know that. I'll remember next time one of my *kinder* gets burned," Sarah said.

"We should take you to the hospital as soon as possible." Eli spoke to Julia, ignoring the comments around him. "I'm afraid you'll experience a bit of pain for a while. Let's keep your hand submerged in the water while we drive you into town."

He glanced at Martin.

"*Ja*, I'll get the buggy." With a sharp nod, Martin sprinted toward the pasture where the road horses were grazing.

"Mar-tin! I wanna come with you. Julia's my girl," Hank called to him.

Martin slowed and glanced over his shoulder, ready to bark an irritated command for his brother to stay behind. He didn't have time to deal with Hank right now and didn't want to argue with the boy.

Thankfully, David clasped Hank's arm and pulled him back. "You'll stay right here with your *mudder* and me, *sohn*. Too many people will slow things down and Eli needs to get Julia to the hospital quickly."

"Ah!" Hank grouched.

Martin hurried on, jumping over the fence surrounding *Mamm*'s vegetable garden. As he passed, his booted heels sank deep into the graveled driveway. He'd get the horse harnessed and ready to go right now.

As he lunged through the gate, the road horses scattered and he forced himself to slow down so he wouldn't spook them. One thought pounded his brain. He had to help Julia. She was hurting badly. He had to get her some relief soon. While he'd watched Eli tending her wounds, he'd felt so helpless. So powerless to do anything for her.

And what would he tell her mother? He was responsible for Julia. It had been his job to keep her safe. He hated the thought of telling Sharon that he had failed.

Now, he had a mission. Something concrete that he could do for her. His horse was well rested and could race him and Eli into town with Julia. They could be at the hospital within twenty-five minutes.

Martin's hands trembled as he harnessed the horse to the buggy. He forced himself to calm down. But he dreaded driving Julia home to her mother afterward. Dreaded the accusing look that would undoubtedly fill Sharon's eyes. She didn't want Julia to come to church with him and look what had happened.

Julia had to be all right. She just had to be. Because nothing else mattered now except her.

Chapter Seven

"Oww!" Julia dropped the bucket of coconut oil on the floor with a thump and cradled her injured hand close against her abdomen. It was midmorning the day after her accident and she was at home, struggling to accomplish her work.

"I thought you were upstairs resting." Sharon came up behind her, picked up the heavy bucket and set it on one of the new industrial-strength shelves Martin had built for her last week.

A strong gust of wind buffeted the front porch but the overhanging canopy didn't budge an inch. Martin's work was quality and she was grateful for his skills. But the leaden clouds filling the sky were a bad premonition and she feared the weather might change before they were able to go into the mountains for firewood. She hated the thought of parting with more precious funds to buy the wood from a vendor in town but they might not have a choice.

"There's too much work to take it easy. I need to accomplish something productive today." Using her right hand, Julia picked up a birchwood mold and stacked it on a shelf with a variety of other wood and silicone molds.

As Eli Stoltzfus had predicted, the doctor had wrapped the burns on her left hand and wrist in loose gauze until she looked like she wore a white boxer's glove. The thick packing helped cushion the wound while it healed but it was cumbersome and difficult to manage. Because her skin had blistered, the wound could become infected. Thankfully, the scald had been superficial and would heal in time for her to make more soap before her deadline…but not soon enough for her.

At least she still had the use of her right hand. But she was stunned to discover just how much she needed two good hands to do her chores. Simple tasks like washing her face or brushing her hair had become difficult. Also, the copious padding of the compress made it rather difficult to do anything with precision. If nothing else, she was fast acquiring compassion for people who had to deal with such disabilities on a permanent basis.

"The doctor said you should take it easy for a few days." Sharon rested a fist on her hip as she stood next to the doorway.

Martin was outside in the parking lot, cutting pieces of gray Formica to finish the countertops. Soon, he would be ready to install the glass partition to separate the workroom from the retail part of the store.

Julia stepped over to the new glass display case she'd purchased secondhand from the grocery store in town. Using her good hand, she dipped a rag into a bucket of hot soapy water, wrung it out as best she could, then scrubbed one of the shelf inserts.

"I'm not an invalid, Mom," she said. "As long as I don't use my left hand, I should be fine. We have a store to get operational. If I sit upstairs all day, we won't be ready for our grand opening the first of December and I'll go stir-crazy."

"Excuse us, please."

Julia turned. Martin and Hank stood in the open doorway holding a long sheet of Formica. Both he and Sharon stepped back as the men carried the heavy piece over to the framework for the new counter and laid it into place.

"That looks *wundervoll*. It should be easy to clean and won't show the grime and dirt at all." Julia eyed the slate-gray Formica with approval.

Sharon frowned. "You're speaking their language now?"

Julia blinked, then nodded. "It's been fun to learn some of their words and phrases." She'd been studying the Scriptures at night and praying, too. For some reason, she had an insatiable desire to learn more about God.

Sharon cast an accusing glance at Martin, biting her bottom lip as if to keep from telling him off. Her animosity toward the Amish man was palpable.

"Aren't you supposed to be upstairs resting?" Martin asked Julia. He wore leather gloves and laid a hand on top of the new countertop.

Lifting her eyebrows in an *I told you so* expression, Sharon peered at her daughter. "You see? Even Martin agrees with me. You should be upstairs."

"I can clean the cabinet for you," Hank offered. He stepped close and took the wash rag from her hand.

"*Danke*, Hank," she said, though she doubted he would be as thorough as her. To make him happy, she would let him clean most of the grime off the shelves, then return later to make sure the job was pristine.

"Go rest and *beheef dich*." Martin nudged her shoulder, urging her away from the cabinet.

"What does that mean?" Julia asked, determined to stay right where she was.

"It means *behave yourself.* Something which you seem to have a lot of trouble doing," Martin said.

Julia laughed, thinking his choice of words quite funny. She was bored upstairs and her mind was racing with all the work needing to be done. With her damaged hand, she wouldn't be able to help Martin go into the mountains to collect firewood. Snow would soon fly and she wasn't sure what they would do without fuel to heat the building. The electrical heating system was certainly of no use to them now. Not without power. If the store got too cold, their customers wouldn't want to visit. But she didn't want to purchase the wood either. So, what could she do?

"That's right. For once, I agree with Martin," Sharon said.

Martin glowered and Julia thought he was angry with her until she saw a twinkle in his eyes and his lips twitched with a suppressed smile. Again, she laughed and repeated the Deitsch phrase, noticing her mother's frown. Obviously, Mom didn't like her learning the Amish language.

"I'm not going upstairs, so stop badgering me. I'm not in pain and there is too much to be done…" She began the argument but never got the chance to finish. "Hey! What is that?" She pointed out the wide sparkling windows that fronted the store.

Pulling into the parking lot and lining up along Main Street were six empty hay wagons pulled by the largest draft horses she'd ever seen. Approximately thirty Amish men accompanied the wagons.

"*Ach*, there's *Daed*!" Hank ran outside to greet his father.

Sure enough, David Hostetler sat in the driver's seat of one big wagon.

"It's a frolic," Martin said.

"A frolic?" Confused by this turn of events, Julia and her mother followed Hank and stood on the front porch. The chill wind buffeted them and Julia folded her arms against the bitter cold.

"*Ja*, a work frolic." Without explaining, Martin went to speak with his father and Bishop Yoder. A number of Amish women hopped down off the wagon seats and headed toward the store.

"Harvest season is over with, so what are they doing here with their wagons?" Rubbing her arms briskly with her hands, Sharon whispered the question to her daughter.

Julia shrugged. "I… I think they're here to get firewood for us."

She was fascinated by the sight. How she longed to ride in one of the wagons pulled by two large Percherons or Belgians. Since she knew little about horses, she wasn't sure what breed they were. She could just imagine Martin driving the big animals as he plowed and planted a hayfield. It sounded fun and exciting to her.

"*Hallo*, Julia." Linda Hostetler waved and smiled pleasantly as she stepped up onto the porch.

Sarah, Naomi, Lizzie and Lori waited nearby, each wearing their black mantle coats and white prayer *kapps* and smiling shyly. Even Marva Geingerich had accompanied the women into town. She stood beside the bishop's wife, her black traveling bonnet pulled low across her face as she gazed at Julia with a severe scowl. Julia chose to ignore the elderly woman. After all, she had done nothing wrong and refused to feel shame simply because Marva disapproved of her.

Holding her injured hand close against her abdomen, Julia stepped down off the porch to greet the women. "*Hallo!* What are you all doing here?"

"We are having a frolic. We have come to help with your work," Linda explained with a wide smile.

Abby Fisher stepped up onto the porch. She smiled sweetly as she handed an apple pie to Sharon before speaking in perfect English. "Hello. This is for you."

"Um, thank you." Sharon nodded, looking stunned and skeptical.

Hank ran over to Julia and handed her a yellow tulip bud that had been in a warm spot of the yard and had just started to bloom. "This is for you, because you're my girl."

The tip of his tongue protruded slightly from between his thick lips as he looked at her with those big, innocent eyes and a silly grin.

She gazed at the flower. "*Danke*, Hank. I'll put it in some water."

She reached out and patted his cheek, smiling as sweetly as she could. Then, she looked at the wagons again and blinked. She'd heard the word *frolic* yesterday at church but didn't understand its meaning. "What's going on? What is a frolic?"

By that time, Martin and Bishop Yoder had joined her.

"It's quite simple," the bishop explained. "You were injured yesterday while protecting little Rachel from the scalding water. Now, you cannot do your own work.

Martin has told us that you have an important deadline coming up, so we have come to help you."

"I... I don't know what to say," Julia said.

"There is nothing to say. While the men go into the mountains to retrieve firewood for you, the *weibsleit* will help get your store ready for your grand opening."

"The *weibsleit*?" she asked.

"The womenfolk," Bishop Yoder explained.

She repeated the word twice, a large lump forming in her throat. A sudden rush of tears filled her eyes and she felt dazed by emotion. These were such good people. She'd never known such generosity. All her life, she'd longed for a large family to love. These people weren't her family but they sure had run to her aid.

"I'm overwhelmed by your kindness but I don't want to take you away from your own work," she said.

Martin stepped closer, his expression gentle, his presence comforting.

"Julia, this is what we do," he said. "We help one another. You saved Rachel and now you are in need. It is our way to assist in any way we can. We want to refresh and comfort you in the midst of your stress."

His explanation touched her heart like nothing else could. She looked at each of the Amish men. Gruff men who wouldn't meet her gaze. Some of them sat in the driver's seats of their wagons, holding the lead lines as they held their horses steady. Others stood in the back of the wagons adjusting a variety of saws, axes, mallets, wedges and other tools they used to cut firewood. They laughed and talked together like this was an ordinary day.

She turned and glanced at the women, who stood just in front of the porch, seeming to wait for an invitation to go inside. At the age of twenty-two, Lori was the youngest and shivered in her woolen mantle. With her petite, pretty features, she looked much too young to be Rachel's mother.

In each man and woman's face, Julia saw no guile or resentment. Nothing but expectation and friendship gleamed in their eyes.

Sharon and Marva were the glaring exceptions. Still holding the pie, Julia's mother gaped at the gathering as if they'd all lost their minds. Her eyes were wide with repugnance, her lips pursed tight. In fact, she looked almost as sour as Marva. Sharon didn't want the Amish here but Julia wasn't in much condition to lift, carry and wash right now. With so many people, the work would go fast. She needed their assistance and it wouldn't be kind or prudent to refuse their offer to help.

"Many hands make light work," Linda pointed out in a kind voice, as if reading her mind.

"*Ja*, and we have Ben to help us today," Bishop Yoder said.

"Ben?" Julia queried.

"Ben Yoder, my nephew. He's visiting us from Bloomfield, Iowa." The bishop turned and pointed at a giant man standing in front of the last wagon. He stood at least four inches taller than Martin, had massive shoulders that seemed wider than a broom handle and looked to be bull strong. For all his enormous size, the young man wore a gentle, unassuming expression and Julia couldn't help liking him on the spot.

"Yes, I see you have a secret weapon," Julia said with a laugh.

Bishop Yoder chuckled. "*Ja*, we have a secret weapon named Ben."

Julia exhaled, deciding to swallow her pride and accept their generous offer.

"*Danke!* This is so kind of you all. My *mudder* and I appreciate your help so much," she said.

"*Wunderbaar!*" the bishop exclaimed. "Martin will remain here to build the shelves you need. The rest of us *mannsleit* will be back this evening with enough wood to last you through the winter."

Mannsleit. Julia assumed that meant *menfolk.*

"One of our wagons will go around back and load up all the garbage you have cleared out of your store and haul it to the dump. The rest of us will go into the mountains for the wood," the bishop said.

Ah, Martin must have explained to the bishop that she had piles of debris in her backyard.

"Next Monday, we'll return to cut up the wood we bring down from the mountain. That evening, you both must join us at my home to enjoy a frolic supper." The bishop glanced between Julia and Sharon, his eyes filled with invitation.

"Um, *danke.* That sounds nice," Julia said, not quite sure she or Mom were up to a party right now.

With a polite nod, the bishop walked over to the lead wagon and climbed into the seat. His return signaled the other men that it was time to leave. They scurried into position. With a loud whistle and a slap of the leather lead lines, Bishop Yoder sent his horses into a steady walk down the middle of Main Street.

Watching them go, Julia noticed several people came out of the general store, post office and bank to watch them pass by. It wasn't every day the townsfolk saw six big wagons pulled by giant horses and filled with Amish men wearing black felt hats drive down the middle of their town. It was an amazing site to behold.

The last wagon in the train peeled off and headed down the alley to Julia's backyard. Two teenage boys drove that wagon and she made a mental note to take them hot chocolate as they cleaned up the debris they would haul off to the garbage dump.

Shivering in the wind, Julia held onto her tulip as she faced the women, still feeling overwhelmed by this generosity.

"You look familiar to me. Do I know you from somewhere?" Marva Geingerich spoke in her loud, gruff voice as she peered shrewdly at Sharon. Marva took a step toward Julia's mom, who still stood on the front porch.

"No, I'm sure you don't. I'm not Amish." Sharon shook her head emphatically. Her face had blanched white and she wouldn't meet Marva's gaze. Without another word, she turned and carried the pie into the store.

"*Ach*, if you'll show us what needs to be done, we'll get to work." Linda sounded all businesslike as she undid her mantle coat and stepped up on the porch.

"Of course." Julia led the women inside, wondering what had gotten into her mother. She was so rude to Martin and his people. She was nowhere in sight and Julia figured she had either returned to their apartment upstairs or gone to work in the back office.

"Hank, will you help me adjust this panel so I can seal it down?" Martin asked.

Out of the corner of her eye, Julia saw him directing Hank to position the length of Formica so it could be secured to the wooden frame of the new counter.

Within minutes, Julia had taken each Amish woman's mantle and stowed them in the office where they wouldn't get sawdust on them. Mom wasn't there so Julia figured she must be upstairs.

Returning to the workroom, Julia directed two women to clean the glass cabinet. She asked another woman to clean an old but charming hutch she had acquired from the secondhand store for showcasing her soaps and lotions.

Linda took up the broom and dustbin and continually swept up sawdust and other debris created by Martin and Hank's work. She fetched and carried, taking some of the burden off Martin.

Marva and Lori sat at a corner table, packaging the lotions and soaps Julia had made for display in the store. Lori used a battery-operated heat gun to shrink a piece of plastic wrap around each bar of soap. Marva peeled off the sticky labels Julia had ordered from an online vendor she'd accessed from a computer at the library and slapped one on each bar of soap. The stickers included the store's rose logo, name and address, and a list of ingredients for each item.

Julia had already mailed off samples of her products to various retail stores in Denver and other major cities throughout the western United States. Hopefully the vendors would place some wholesale orders for her soaps. Always helpful, Carl Nelson had given her a referral to a reputable sales representative out of Denver. Julia had written to them, hoping they could help market her goods.

With everyone occupied with a task, Julia soon found that she had little to do. Martin stepped outside to cut another piece of wood. Hank had gotten distracted and was fiddling with a pair of scissors at the packing table.

"Give those to me, boy. You're going to cut your hand off," Marva snapped at him as she jerked the scissors away.

Ignoring the women, Julia stepped outside to speak with Martin for a moment.

"Did you coordinate all of this?" she asked him.

He glanced up at her before laying a narrow piece of oak across the two sawhorses he'd set up in the parking lot. Using a measuring tape, he calculated the length and drew a tiny line with a pencil he kept tucked behind his ear. Picking up his handsaw, he smiled.

"*Ja*, but it was Lori's idea for the women to help. I told her about your work and she knew you needed to be up and running so you can make soap just after Thanksgiving. Since you'd lost the use of your left hand, she asked Bishop Yoder if she might come and help." He shrugged his broad shoulders. "I also mentioned you needed firewood. One thing led to another. The bishop said we must have a work frolic. So, here we are."

He made a quick cut with the handsaw, then peered at her. "Honestly, I think Bishop Yoder is highly motivated to help you all he can."

"Oh? And why is that?"

"You should know that he hopes you'll become Amish. Since you showed an interest in our faith, they all think that is your intention."

She laughed at that. "I do like your people very much, Martin. But I doubt I'll ever join your faith. My mom doesn't approve and I don't want to do anything to upset her."

He hesitated and licked his bottom lip. The teasing sparkle left his eyes and he ducked his head over his work. "That is most unfortunate."

Oh, dear. She didn't want to upset him either.

"You should still join us at the Bishop's *heemet* for the frolic supper next Monday," he said. "It'll be a potluck with everyone bringing lots of food, and if the weather holds, we will play baseball."

"Baseball? But I can't hold a bat or glove." She held up her bandaged hand. She hadn't played the game since she'd been a child in school. The thought of playing with friends was tantalizing.

"*Ach*, that is no deterrent. I will bat for you and you can run the bases. Since I'll already be working here, I can drive you and your *mudder* to the bishop's farm that afternoon, then bring you home again," he said.

"I'm afraid *Mamm* won't want to go," she said.

"That's all right. She is invited anyway."

She laughed, thinking it might be loads of fun. Martin was just a friend so what could it hurt? "I'm amazed by the kindness of your people. No one has ever been so good, er, *gut* to me and my *mudder*. *Danke*, Martin. Though I don't want to become Amish, I'll be sure to invite all of you to our grand opening on the first of December."

He looked up and flashed that devastating smile of his, but a sad quality had replaced the gaiety she'd seen there moments before. Was he truly disappointed that she didn't want to become Amish? And why should it matter so much to him?

"I'm sure they will like that," he said.

He returned to work and she went inside, her heart and mind full of emotions she couldn't name. She liked these Amish people. She really did. Especially Martin. Most of them were kind, welcoming and helpful. In fact, Julia was inclined to ask if she could attend church again. She admitted to herself that she wanted to learn more. The Scriptures she'd been reading only gave her more inquiries. And because of her injury, she never got the opportunity to ask Martin all the questions she had acquired at church yesterday.

Just one problem: Sharon. Her mom didn't like the Amish. She didn't want Julia to go to church or learn their language. Maybe Mom feared Julia might fall in love and want to marry Martin. But that didn't make sense. Mom had always told her she could love and wed anyone she chose. So, what was the issue? Why was Mom so against anything to do with the Amish?

Glancing out the window, Julia paused for a few moments to admire the way Martin's blue chambray shirt tightened across the heavy muscles of his back. He was such a tall, strong man. So generous and capable. A man much like Julia's father. Someone to be admired. And for the first time since she'd met him, she wished Martin wasn't Amish.

But it wouldn't matter. Dallin had taught her never to trust another man with her heart. No matter what, she could never be anything more than friends with Martin. And that was that.

"I don't know why you're being so rude to the Amish. It isn't like you to act that way."

Martin stepped to the end of the hallway and paused when he heard the words coming from the back office in a low murmur. Though he couldn't see her, he knew Julia's voice and she sounded upset.

"I don't want you to marry that man, that's why." Sharon's unmistakable voice lifted in a harsh whisper.

Yes, it was Julia and her mother speaking and they were discussing him. Martin took another step and they came into view. Their backs were turned so they didn't notice him.

"I'm not going to marry anyone, Mom. Not after what Dallin did to me. Martin and I are just friends. You have no call to treat him and his people with anything but respect," Julia said.

"Yes, you're friends. Until you fall in love with him."

"Mom, that's not going to happen."

"Maybe not yet but what if your friendship blossoms into something more? That's how it happens when you fall in love. And then, what will you do? If you don't join his faith, he'll be shunned if he marries you. Is that what you want for him? He'd lose everything. His family wouldn't speak to him. He'd be completely ostracized. And you! If you join the Amish, they'll dominate and run your life. They might not even let you visit me because I'm *Englisch*."

"Oh, Mom!" Julia cried in a harsh breath. "Don't be so dramatic. They know you're my mother and that you're ill with lupus. Of course they'd let me visit and take care of you. Besides, I'm not joining the Amish, and Martin isn't leaving his faith. We aren't going to fall in love and we certainly aren't going to get married. So, there's nothing to fret about."

Sharon paused several moments, looking at her daughter. "I still don't want them here. We don't need their help."

"They're a blessing. I don't understand why you're so against them." Julia shook her head, seeming stunned by how unreasonable her mother was being.

Sharon simply pursed her lips tighter.

The floorboards creaked beneath Martin's booted foot and a gasp followed by dead silence filled the air.

He hesitated, ready to go back the way he had come. But too late. The two women turned at the open doorway.

"Martin!" Julia said.

"Ahem! Excuse me, but the *mannsleit* have returned. They have already cut most of the logs and even split some of the wood into smaller pieces of kindling that are perfect for your wood-burning stoves. They'll return on Monday to finish it. They would come back tomorrow but they need a little time to work at their own farms. They're stacking what they've finished neatly in your backyard right now and have piled it far away from your house, so you don't end up with termites." He tried to speak normally but his throat felt like a wad of sandpaper had lodged there. It would be dishonest to pretend he hadn't overheard their conversation. His face flooded with heat and he felt awkward and embarrassed to be caught eavesdropping.

Sharon glared at him with censure. Brushing past him, she went upstairs.

Julia showed a nervous smile. Since she'd been caught talking about him, Martin wasn't surprised.

"I can't believe they got all that work done in one day," Julia said.

He showed an uncertain smile. "They all worked together to get it done."

Julia stepped out into the hallway with him and headed toward the back door. Martin followed, grateful to get away from Sharon.

Standing on the back porch, they observed the Amish men for several minutes. Long logs of aspen and ponderosa pine lay off to the side of the spacious yard, cleaned of all their stubby branches and ready for splitting into smaller chunks. Near the house lay a small pile of split wood, all ready for taking into the house to be consumed by the old black stoves.

As if on cue, the men stopped working, dusted off their shirts and pants and reached for their jackets. Carrying their axes and saws on their shoulders, they headed toward the front of the house, nodding politely as they passed.

Julia waved farewell. "They did so much work. I'm overwhelmed and very relieved to have this done."

"*Ja*, they're going *heemet* now for supper. The aspen burns hotter than the pine and is good for starting fires. The men will return next Monday to finish splitting the wood. Then we'll go to the bishop's house for supper that evening. That's part of a frolic. Lots of fun work and *gut* food."

She lifted her eyebrows in question. "I'm surprised to hear you call hard work fun. Most people don't like work. But the Amish seem to be the exception."

He frowned. "*Ja*, we enjoy what we accomplish with our own two hands. You like hard work, don't you?"

She nodded. "It's how we get what we need to live. And it gives me a sense of accomplishment."

"It's a blessing to serve. By the time the men are finished, you should have enough firewood to last through the winter," Martin said.

She paused, thinking this over. "I just realized something."

"What is that?" he asked.

"The Amish faith isn't an individual, solitary religion. It's a community of members serving one another, looking after each other and seeing to one another's needs. Isn't that right?"

A wide smile split his handsome face. "*Ja*, you do understand after all. We rely on one another for everything. Our *Gmay* is more than just the individual members of our Amish community. It is also the rules we follow, our social structure and how we look after each other."

She nodded, a pensive frown tugging at her forehead. "And you have extended that honor to me simply because I came to your church and protected little Rachel from being burned?"

He shook his head. "*Ne*, you are not a member of our *Gmay*. Not unless you accept our *Ordnung* and are baptized into our faith. Our beliefs permeate every aspect of our life. For my people, *Gott* speaks through our community and we are guided by submitting ourselves to the wisdom of the *Gmay*. But we also believe in serving others in any way we can. And you and your *mudder* were in need."

She nodded. "I see."

"Bishop Yoder is still hoping your *mudder* will join us at the frolic supper next week," Martin said.

She frowned and scuffed the tip of her tennis shoe against the wooden porch. Perhaps he shouldn't have reminded her but the bishop had instructed him to do so. And he wouldn't dream of defying Bishop Yoder.

Sharon was not happy to have her daughter involved with the Amish. And Julia had made it clear she had no intention of joining their faith. But what if Julia changed her mind? What if she just needed a bit more time to get to know the Amish better? Perhaps her heart could be softened and her mind could be changed. It had happened before.

"Even if my *mudder* decides not to go, I definitely want to," she said.

A blaze of joy flashed through his chest. "*Gut*. I'll

tell my *vadder* and the bishop that you'll be joining us." He nodded, forcing himself not to laugh out loud with delight. "I had best get *heemet* now. But I'll be back in the morning as usual."

She nodded with understanding. "*Ja*, I'll see you to-morrow."

As he turned away and headed around to the front of the house to find Hank, he felt a bit of doubt. She had said yes and wanted to go to the frolic supper, but her words to her mother still rang in his ears. She had no intention of becoming Amish.

Once he finished his job here, he wouldn't see her anymore. No more teaching her Deitsch. No more work-ing, planning and laughing together. And somehow that made him feel sad and empty inside.

Chapter Eight

On Monday the following week, Julia awoke to the thunk of axes and the burr of saws. Rising from her bed, she slid the curtains open just a bit and gazed out. Shimmering sunlight gleamed against the frost covering the barren trees. A nest of dried orange and yellow leaves carpeted the ground. She really must find time to rake them up before it snowed.

At least two dozen men swarmed her backyard, cutting the long logs into smaller stumps. It had been a week since they had brought the firewood down from the mountains. Tonight, when their chore was done, they would enjoy the frolic supper at Bishop Yoder's farm. And Julia couldn't wait.

She paused beside the dresser in her room, running her fingertips over the pages of her Bible. She'd been reading the Scriptures every spare moment she could find. The passages filled her heart with warmth and gave her a sense of something greater than herself. Accompanied by prayer, her faith and relationship with God was growing more every day.

Hurrying to dress, she dragged a comb through her

long hair, tied it into a jaunty ponytail and raced downstairs. When she stepped to the back door, she found Mom standing there. Dressed in her long pajamas and bathrobe, she was watching the men through the screen door.

"You're up early," Julia said with a smile.

"Not as early as them. Their women woke me up and I let them into the store." Mom nodded at the Amish.

Julia gasped. "The women returned, too?"

"Yes. Three of them. They brought us a fresh loaf of bread and an apple cobbler."

"That was nice of them. Who all is here?"

Sharon shrugged. "I don't know their names."

"Mom! Of course you do. They were each introduced to you last week. You should try to be nicer to them." Julia hated to admonish her own mother but still couldn't fathom her discourtesy.

"How are you feeling?" Julia asked, trying to change the topic. She wrapped an arm around Mom's waist and leaned against her in an affectionate hug. She'd had a bad attack over the past few days and Julia was worried about her.

"I'm fine." Mom squeezed her back.

"Did you remember to take your medication this morning?" With the cooler weather, Mom's joint and muscle pain had increased. Julia knew she hadn't been sleeping well either. Maybe it was time to make another appointment with the doctor in town. He was an older gentleman who had retired here to Riverton but still opened up his office two days per week. A blessing for them.

"Of course."

"Good. Getting the soap store operational isn't as important as you are," Julia said.

Another tight hug and Mom released her. "The Amish certainly are persistent. I didn't think they'd return."

Her voice held an edge of grudging respect and a bit of resentment, too.

"The Amish can be generous as long as you don't cross them. But I can't help wondering at their motives," Mom said.

Julia shrugged one shoulder. "As far as I know, they want nothing from us."

"Hmm," came Mom's skeptical reply.

Julia went very still. She couldn't help thinking the Amish were like the large family she'd always wished for. They were there when she needed them, ready to help in any way possible. And tonight, she would go to the frolic supper and play baseball and have fun with them.

"They haven't asked us for anything, Mom. We don't have much to offer. What could they possibly want?" she asked.

"You," Mom said.

The word was like a slap to her face. It caused Julia to take a quick inhale. She forced herself not to shudder. Her mother's comment seemed a bit sinister. Surely Martin's people weren't that manipulative and conniving.

"I'm not going to become Amish, so you can relax on that point," Julia insisted.

Mom jutted her chin toward the door. "Do they know that? Does Martin know?"

"Yes, I told him. And he tells his parents almost everything, so they all know."

Mom snorted. "The Amish don't take no for an answer."

"Martin is my employee. He's here to do a job. That's all. It won't hurt us to be nice to him."

"I hope you're right," Mom said.

Julia gazed out into the yard. Several men took turns using a two-handled saw to cut the logs into stumps with long, even strokes. Wielding axes, more men rolled the stumps over to a large cutting block where a chisel was used to split the stumps into hand-size chunks of kindling. Each man seemed to know when it was his turn to chop and when to rest. Their happy banter and laughter carried through the air.

"Julia, can I get your opinion on something?"

She turned and found Martin standing at the end of the hallway. His tall silhouette almost blocked the rays of sunshine that glistened at his back.

Without a word, Sharon slipped away and Julia went to greet him. As they walked into the retail part of the store, Julia glanced over and saw Linda and Lori stocking the shelves. Again, she was embarrassed to find them here working while she'd been upstairs sleeping.

Both women knelt on the floor as they slid narrow boxes of homemade lip balms and lotions into the display case. Thankfully, the products had been made long before Julia's hand had been burned.

The low murmur of their voices seemed so comforting to her. Even though it had been such a short time, she felt as though she knew these women well and they were good friends. Surely her mother's fears were unwarranted.

"Guder mariye," she called in a pleasant tone.

"Hallo, Julia." Linda waved.

Lori nodded and showed a shy smile.

"Do you like how we are displaying your notions?" Linda asked.

Julia glanced at the shelves, noticing how the women had lined up each bottle so the labels were front and center. The variety of soaps caused a spicy-sweet scent to fill the air. The light pink and lavender creams looked so appealing that she felt certain the local ranchers' wives wouldn't be able to resist them. At least, that was what she hoped.

"It's perfect. And don't forget to bring in some of your rag rugs. I've got a cute display rack that will be great for showing off your work," Julia said.

"*Ja*, a number of us women are working on them. We're glad to have the extra income. I'll bring them in time for your grand opening." Linda beamed with pleasure.

Good. Now if only Julia could get the large soap orders made before her deadline. Other than her mother's health, that was her greatest concern right now.

"Take a look at this." Martin gestured toward her workroom. She was surprised to see David Hostetler standing nearby, his work-roughened hands folded beneath his black suspenders. He smiled but didn't speak.

Julia gasped at what she saw. Rising from the Formica countertop, a frameless tempered glass partition reached clear up to the ceiling and separated the retail side of the store from the workroom where she would make her soap. With the glass panel to separate the two rooms, no noxious fumes of lye would bother her customers. Martin's craftsmanship looked perfect and very professional.

"The glass was so large and unwieldy that *Daed*

helped me hold it steady while I installed it this morning. I didn't want to take the chance that I might crack the glass while working alone," Martin said.

"I helped, too," Hank chimed in from across the room. As usual, he hurried over to Julia, standing a bit too close as he grinned up at her.

She smiled back.

Martin reached out and ruffled the boy's hair in a loving gesture. "*Ja*, Hank helped a lot. So, what do you think of it, Jules?"

Jules! No one had ever called her that before. With Martin's foreign accent, the name sounded rather exotic. His deep, low voice caused a little shiver of delight to run up her spine. She paused, repeating the name silently in her mind.

"I'm sorry, Julia. I shouldn't have called you that. It just slipped out. I don't know where I even got it from," he said.

She laughed. "It's okay. I kind of like it." Actually, she was glad he felt relaxed enough around her to give her a nickname.

He flashed a smile. "You do?"

She nodded, a hard lump rising in her throat. With the bright sun blazing through the wide windows, he looked so handsome standing there. She didn't have the heart to object. All her life, she'd dreamed of having friends. She'd dreamed of having her own business, too. Seeing all of Martin's hard work and the partition now in place made that dream a reality.

"Ahem! We'll be having the frolic supper this evening. Will your *mudder* be joining us?" David cleared his throat, breaking into her fanciful thoughts.

"*Ne*, she doesn't feel up to going," she said.

Her face flushed with heat and she stepped toward the glass, trying to hide her embarrassment. She couldn't believe she'd actually been flirting with Martin in front of his father, of all people!

"Do you really like it?" Martin asked again from behind.

She nodded quickly, hardly able to speak. "It's perfect. It's just what I always dreamed of."

"I helped clean the glass." Hank followed her, lifting a roll of paper towels and a bottle of glass cleaner that had been sitting on the table.

"I see you did a good job, too. *Danke* for all your work," Julia said.

Hank smiled so brightly that she thought a zillion sunbeams must have exploded inside his head.

Julia turned toward David. "And *danke* to you, as well."

"It's my pleasure." The older man smiled politely and ducked his head.

"I'll get the stove and fridge installed later this afternoon. *Daed* will help the men outside, then go *heemet* to do his work before the frolic supper tonight," Martin said.

She glanced at David, noticing his calm, friendly gaze. If only she knew what he was thinking. He was Martin's father and for some crazy reason, she desperately wanted his approval.

"I can't tell you how grateful I am for all your help. I feel so bad that you've left your own chores at home in order to come to my aid," she told him.

"It's no problem. You saved our little Rachel, so it's the least we can do to help you." David spoke in an even tone, yet he seemed a bit guarded. After all, she was *Englisch* whether she was interested in his faith or not.

"Kumme helfe cut the firewood, Hank." Picking up a bucket of rags, David glanced at his younger son.

"But I want to stay here with Julia," Hank whined.

"Ne, you will *komm* with me now." As if expecting the boy to obey, the man walked outside.

With a backward glance at her, Hank followed begrudgingly. Through the wide windows fronting the store, Julia watched the two of them walk around the house to the backyard. She figured they would help the other men stack wood. From the looks of things, they'd be finished soon.

"I've almost completed my work here," Martin spoke softly.

Julia jerked, surprised to find him standing right next to her. A feeling of sadness pulsed over her. Once he was finished, she wouldn't see him anymore.

"May I attend your church services again?" The moment she asked, she wondered if she would regret it. She didn't want to give him the impression she was going to join his faith, nor did she want any more contention with her mother. But she couldn't seem to help herself. She really wanted to go.

"Abselutt," he said with a smile.

She tilted her head in question and he explained.

"Absolutely. I will pick you up and drive you this coming Sunday. This time, it will be held at the Fishers' farm."

"I'll bring a casserole to help with the lunch," she said.

"I'm sure they will appreciate that."

She nodded, then looked at the partition again, trying

to ignore the feeling of butterflies swarming her stomach. "I hope the appliances work okay."

She had taken Martin's advice and her appliances would not be powered by electricity.

"They will work fine. You're using gas appliances upstairs in your apartment now. Propane and compressed air can drive your fridge and stove top just as well as electricity," he said.

Out of necessity, she would have to trust Martin's judgment. After what Dallin had put her through, it was a big leap of faith for her. But Martin hadn't let her down yet. And even if the electricity went out again, she'd still be able to power her appliances. That was a big plus.

She stepped through the open doorway to her workroom, running her fingertips over the smooth Formica counters. The oak cabinets and drawers were lovely. There wasn't a bit of dust or grime anywhere to be seen. The white paint she'd applied to the walls gave the room a clinical, sterile appearance, which was perfect in case she had an unannounced FDA inspection to ensure her business was compliant with the law.

She admired the gleaming stainless steel sink and new water faucet Martin had installed. It was a tall, swan's neck spout that loomed high over the sink with plenty of room for her large stockpots to rest inside the basin below. The arch of the faucet would make cleanup much easier.

She turned and smiled at Martin. He stood in the threshold, his strong arms braced over his head against the doorjamb, his right ankle crossed over the left. It was a completely male stance that reminded her what a strong, capable man he was.

And attractive, too.

Shaking her head, she tried to focus on her work. A slight frown tugged at his forehead. He looked worried. No doubt he was concerned she might not like his work.

"It's beautiful. Exactly what I envisioned," she said.

His facial features softened. "I should have everything completed by Thanksgiving. That will give you plenty of time to meet your soap making deadline."

A laugh of relief broke from her throat and she held up her left hand. "*Ja*, I'm cutting it kind of close. I'll get the bandages removed the day after Thanksgiving and plan to make soap right afterward."

Lowering his arms, he stepped nearer and gently touched the thick gauze on her hand. Though she could barely feel his touch, she felt mesmerized by his closeness as she looked up at him.

"Even though the bandages will be removed soon, your hand may be weak from lack of use," he said. "I will be here that afternoon to help you make soap. I can lift the pans off the stove and pour the batter into the molds. I don't want you or your *mudder* to have to lift those heavy pans."

She nodded, realizing he was right. And frankly, she'd gotten used to him being around. She would miss him when he was gone. "*Danke.* I would appreciate it. You've been so great, Martin. I couldn't have done all of this without you and Hank and your people."

"As my *vadder* said, it's our pleasure." With a dip of his head, he reached for his toolbox and busied himself with tidying things up.

Feeling odd and out of place in her own store, she left him to his work. Stepping back into the sales room, she caught the low murmur of the women's voices. One of them laughed and she drew near. Their camaraderie and friendship had become dear to her and she couldn't wait to attend the frolic supper with Martin later that afternoon.

"It'll be nice to have a new member join our *Gmay*," Abby said.

With her back turned toward Julia, Abby sat with Lori and Linda at the worktable. They were cutting lengths of thin grosgrain ribbon to tie around the lip balms and didn't notice she was there.

"*Ja*, once Julia converts, she will make a good *fraa* for Martin. You must be excited to have a new *schwardochder*." Lori smiled at Linda.

Fraa? Schwardochder? Julia's ears perked up at the two unknown words. Hmm, she'd have to ask Martin what they meant, but she feared she already knew.

Like a bolt of lightning, Mom's words rushed through her head. Was it possible Martin's people were only being kind because they hoped to nab her as a new convert to their faith? And what if they found out she had no intention of joining them?

A sick feeling settled in her stomach. Julia hated to disappoint Martin and his family. And once again, those old feelings of hurt and betrayal came crashing in on her. Dallin and Debbie had lied and used her. They'd taught her to distrust people.

She wasn't going to convert to the Amish faith simply because they had chopped her wood and helped in her store. She had to know deep within her heart that the Amish faith was true. She would only convert if she believed in their religion with all her heart. For whatever reasons, Mom didn't approve of the Amish and didn't want them here. Though she'd always longed for siblings and a family of her own, Julia loved her mother most of all. She would never do something to defy or alienate her mom. No, not ever.

Besides, Martin hadn't spoken of marriage to her. They weren't even romantically involved. They were just good friends. Weren't they? That was all they could ever be. Because she was *Englisch* and he was Amish.

But what if his family and the rest of his congregation had made incorrect assumptions about her relationship with Martin? What if they thought she was going to marry him?

She'd have to broach the subject with Martin. But if he thought she was going to join his Amish faith and abandon her mother, he was dead wrong.

"Have you invited Julia to church on Sunday?"

Martin whirled around and found his mother standing nearby, leaning against a sturdy broom. She spoke in Deitsch.

He had just set the giant mixer into place in the workroom and was wiping off a splotch of grease from the large stainless steel bowl. Julia was in the retail part of the store, painting the trim on an old chest of drawers. The chore was perfect for her since it didn't require the use of her injured hand. It was early afternoon—almost time to leave for the frolic supper.

"I… I didn't have to. She asked if she could *komm*." Even though he was a grown man, he felt tongue-tied on this subject.

"*Ach*, that's *gut*," Linda said.

Something hardened inside of Martin. He didn't want to get his hopes up that Julia would join his faith.

"*Mamm*, you mustn't expect too much," he said. "I don't want to push Julia. She's told me her *mudder* doesn't approve and she has no intention of joining our faith."

Linda nodded wisely, her cheeks plumping with her smile. "And yet, she asked if she can *komm* to church again. That means she is interested. So, we shall see. The *gut* Lord works in mysterious ways. Julia may receive a conviction of the truth without intending to. Only time will tell."

Linda turned and reached for her black traveling bonnet and heavy shawl. "We're going *heemet* now, to pick up the other *kinder* and my casserole dish. I'll see you at the bishop's farm for supper."

He nodded but didn't speak as she called to the other women. They came at once, bidding Julia a cheery farewell. Setting her paintbrush aside, she hugged each one in turn. It seemed odd that they were all such good friends, yet Julia insisted she didn't want to become one of them.

Stepping outside, he saw the men had gathered most of their tools and were climbing into their buggies to go home. Their laughter mingled with the mild breeze. Hank was with his father, though the boy was arguing just now. Martin could hear him complaining that he wanted to stay with Julia.

"You'll see her at the frolic supper later on. Now *komm*," David said.

Thankfully, the boy went willingly. Martin suspected his father had purposefully taken Hank with him, to give Martin time alone with Julia. His parents hadn't said so but he knew they hoped Julia would be baptized and Martin would marry her. Funny how they accepted Julia now that they thought she would join their faith. He just hated to disappoint them.

Waving goodbye, Martin rounded the house to the backyard. For some reason, he wanted to be alone for a while. Several tidy piles of firewood had been set back away from the house. All the wood had been cut except for one cord of tree stumps. The men had left that work for Martin to finish.

Lifting the chisel and ax, he placed them on a stump and brought the ax down hard. The crack of the wood sounded in the air as he split it into hand-size pieces. The physical labor felt good and before long, he had to remove his warm coat.

"It's hard work, huh?"

Martin jerked around and found Julia behind him, a safe distance away from the ax. Sitting on a tree stump, she gestured to the scattered wood he'd tossed aside until he was finished and ready to stack it in a pile.

He smiled, not minding the work at all. "*Ja*, but very worth the effort."

"My father told me once that firewood warms you twice. When you cut it and when you use it to heat the house."

Embedding the steel of his ax into the stump, he rested his forearm on the wooden handle. He chuckled, the sound coming deep from within his chest. "*Ja*, your *vadder* was a wise man."

"What does *fraa* mean?" she asked suddenly.

He tilted his head, wondering where she'd heard the word. Probably from one of the women inside. "It means wife."

"And what does *schwardochder* mean?"

"Daughter-in-law," he said.

"Oh, I was afraid of that." She frowned, looking down at the ground.

"Is something wrong?" he asked.

She shook her head but wouldn't meet his eyes. "*Ne*, nothing is wrong. Nothing at all. It's just that I overheard the women talking today and…and… Martin, do your people think you and I are a couple? That we're more than friends?"

She spoke in a rush, her face flushing red. Martin stared, taken aback by her blunt question.

"I'm not sure what they think." He spoke truthfully, feeling suddenly at a loss for something intelligent to say.

"What about your parents? What does your *mudder* think?"

Here it was, the topic he'd been avoiding. It was an odd situation, really. Julia was his employer. She had hired him to do a job. And because she had saved little Rachel from being scalded, his people had come to her aid at the soap store. But they were just friends. They couldn't be anything more.

Could they?

"My *mudder* wishes I would marry but she knows you are *Englisch*," he said.

"And my mom wants me to remain *Englisch*," she said.

"*Ja*, it seems both our *midder* are at cross purposes. But they only want what they believe is best for each of us."

"*Midder?*" she asked.

"One *mudder*, two *midder*," he explained.

She nodded, repeating the new word. Each time he gave her a new Deitsch word, she seemed to remember it easily. And over the past couple of weeks, they had been adding more and more complicated words and phrases to her dialogue. She was now able to piece together simple sentences.

"My *mudder* believes that women are treated like chattel by your men. She thinks Amish women are no more than servants to their husbands and that their entire life is filled with drudgery." Her eyes were filled with sadness, as if she hoped this wasn't true.

He snorted and reached for his coat, sliding his arms into the sleeves before shrugging it up around his shoulders.

"I can't speak for what goes on in other Amish homes, but my *mamm* is definitely not a servant to my *vadder*. He calls her his queen and treats her well. He counsels with her and they make plans together. He seeks her opinion on all matters. *Mamm* and my sisters help in the barn, shop and field. Likewise, my *daed*, brothers and I help in the garden and around the house. I have even hung laundry. Once I marry, I plan to treat my *fraa* the same way."

She nodded. "Okay. Thank you for that explanation."

"Honestly, I think my *vadder* is more afraid of *Mamm* than he is of the bishop. And that is saying a lot," he said.

She laughed, the sound high and sweet. It seemed to melt the frigid ice of their conversation. But in his heart of hearts, Martin couldn't imagine ever abusing Julia or any woman. In fact, the thought of someone hurting her made his chest tighten and his hands tremble. He was a pacifist and had been taught to turn the other cheek but he truly didn't know what he would do if he ever caught someone abusing Julia.

A door slammed somewhere inside the house and she jerked her head in that direction. "It's getting late."

He flashed a smile. "*Ja*, we should leave for the supper."

She stood and turned toward the house. "If you'll give me a few minutes, I'd like to change out of my dirty work clothes."

He nodded. "When you're ready."

Watching her go, his thoughts were a jumble of turmoil. She was curious about his faith but had no intention of converting. *Mamm* thought she might be convinced otherwise. But Martin would not force her. She would have to come to his faith of her own free will. Otherwise, she could change her mind later on down the road. Years could pass and then they'd have disastrous consequences. It must be her choice alone.

Tugging the ax free of the tree stump, he put it away in the shed so the damp weather wouldn't cause it to rust. His father had taught him to be fastidious and careful in everything he did. It was who he was. And in choosing the woman who would one day be his wife, he could be no different.

He walked to the front of the house and leaned against the porch railing as he waited for Julia. She was so different from the Amish girls he knew. So independent. He wasn't sure he could get along with such a woman. In the Amish faith, wives were partners with their husbands but the man had the final word on important issues.

But something had changed between him and Julia today. Something he couldn't quite put his finger on. They had actually discussed having a deeper relationship. But that wasn't possible. They were only friends and nothing more.

Chapter Nine

"They're here! They're here!"

Julia heard Hank's cry from clear across the yard as Martin turned his horse into the pasture. As they walked toward Bishop Yoder's farmhouse, she saw the boy running toward them, his short stocky legs moving as fast as they could go.

Since her left hand was still bandaged, she had let Martin carry her ham-and-potato-cheese casserole for her. Though they only had another hour or so of sunlight left before it got dark, the November day was crisp yet pleasant. The perfect evening for a fall frolic.

"Mar-tin and Julia!"

Hank cried their names over and over until he reached them. Though he didn't touch her, he immediately sidled up next to Julia.

"You're finally here," he said, panting and sweating from his exertions.

"*Hallo*, Hank. *Wie bischt du?*" She smiled at the boy.

"I am *gut*! But we've been waiting for you and I'm about half starved." He skipped along like a little child rather than a fifteen-year-old boy.

Julia laughed at his melodramatic statement. "I'm sorry we're late."

"*Ach*, it's *allrecht*. We can eat now you're here." Hank flashed a good-natured grin in spite of the loud rumblings of his stomach.

Children raced across the yard in a game of chase while the teenage youths bunched together to discuss their day. The gathering was just like that on Church Sunday, except that everyone still wore their work clothes. But no one was eating. They were obviously waiting for her and Martin.

"Is the entire *Gmay* here?" Julia spoke low to Martin.

"*Ja*, and they're happy to see you," he said.

Julia wasn't so sure. The men sat at the tables or stood talking in clusters while the women bustled about setting out food. Since she'd attended one of their church gatherings and had worked with many of them at her soap studio, Julia knew most of them by name.

"I hope they're not irritated to be kept waiting," she said.

"*Ne*, of course not. You are their guest of honor. They only wish your *mudder* could be here, too," he said.

She stumbled over the uneven ground. Holding the casserole with one hand, Martin shot out his free hand to steady her. He just as quickly released her but not before she felt his firm, strong fingers around her arm.

Realizing his people were watching, Julia felt a flush of embarrassment. "Many of them have been working at my place all day. I would think they'd be sick of me by now."

Martin shook his head. "*Ne*, that isn't our way. *Gott* expects us to care for and serve one another."

His words touched her deeply. Was he for real? His attitude seemed so different from Dallin's. Whenever she'd asked her ex-fiancé for help, he'd done so begrudgingly. Not with a willing heart and a smile. "I don't know how to ever repay them."

"No payment is necessary."

His words reminded her of a scripture she'd read last night about when Jesus gave His apostles a new commandment to love one another as they loved themselves. "Then you will just have to let me know when you have another work frolic and I will be there to help."

He smiled at that. "*Gut!* I am glad to see you understand how hard work can bless everyone."

As they reached the group, Julia saw that they all looked tired from their day's labors but they didn't complain and they all wore happy smiles on their faces. Yes, Julia understood what they were feeling. It was the fatigue and the joy of accomplishing wonderful things that day. She decided then that she loved the Amish work ethic.

"*Hallo!*" several of them called to her.

Julia smiled and waved, then immediately went to help the women lay out the meal. They welcomed her like a long-lost friend. Since it was a potluck, everyone had brought food items to contribute to the feast. A variety of casseroles, pickled beets, breads and pies were arrayed on the long tables. Julia pointed to where Martin should set her casserole, happy that she had contributed to the meal.

"That looks delicious." Linda nodded at the dish and hugged Julia.

Feeling happy inside, Julia smiled and returned the woman's embrace. "*Danke*, but I can't take credit. My *mudder* made it. She wanted me to pass on my thanks to all of you."

Linda drew back in surprise, her eyes wide, her mouth curving in a smile. "*Ach*, your *mudder* made the casserole? That was nice of her."

"*Ja*, very nice." Several other women stood nearby, nodding in approval.

"But she didn't want to join us?" Lori asked.

"*Ne*, I'm afraid she isn't feeling well."

"I'm sorry to hear she is sick," Abby said.

"She has *gut* days and bad days. I'll let her know you asked about her," Julia said.

"How is your hand?" Eli Stoltzfus stood up from the table to greet her and nodded at the bandages.

"*Gut*. I get the bandages off the day after Thanksgiving. Thanks to you, the doctor believes I will have very little scarring," she said.

"The thanks should be to *Gott*," Eli said, his gaze direct yet humble.

Julia nodded in understanding. She was gradually learning that the Amish were a meek people who didn't seek praise. It was their way to give all the credit to God, which was just one more thing she liked about them. More and more, she was coming to realize the Lord wanted them to serve one another.

"Let us pray," Bishop Yoder called in a loud voice to get everyone's attention.

They each went very quiet and bowed their heads, even the small children. After the prayer, they ate their meal. Martin came to sit next to Julia and she felt instantly relieved. Somehow his presence eased her fears. She was worried about upsetting her mother, yet she also wanted to please herself.

"Vie gehts?" he asked low.

"I am fine. Don't worry so much," she responded.

He smiled at that. She was trying to reassure him, yet she still felt a little uncertain.

"Do you have plans for Thanksgiving dinner?" he asked.

She nodded. *"Ja*, my *mudder* always roasts a turkey."

"Just the two of you?" Linda asked from behind as she reached past them to fill their glasses with water.

"Yes, just us two," Julia said, wishing her father was still here.

"You could join us, if you like. We have plenty of room," Linda said.

"Oh, thank you. But my mother looks forward to cooking every year." Knowing her mother would never agree to having dinner with Martin's family, Julia forgot to speak Deitsch. She was grateful when Linda didn't push the issue.

As Julia ate, she met Martin's gaze. The two of them didn't need to speak for her to know exactly what he was thinking. He was worried about her. He wanted her to feel happy and comfortable among his people. And she did, for the most part.

"Where did you say you were from, girl?"

Julia looked up and saw Marva Geingerich sitting across the table from her. "I'm from Kansas."

Marva narrowed her eyes, her forehead crinkled in a deep frown. "And who are your people?"

Julia forced herself not to stutter as she responded to the old matriarch. She always got the feeling that this woman didn't like her and that made her feel uncomfortable. "My parents are Walter and Sharon Rose. You met my mother last week."

"Hmm. And what was your *mudder*'s maiden name?" Marva asked.

"Miller," Julia said, trying not to bristle at this interrogation.

"Miller?" Marva's lips thinned with disapproval. "I knew a lot of Millers among the Amish when I lived in Ohio."

"Miller is a fairly common name. My *mudder* isn't Amish and I don't think she ever lived in Ohio," Julia said, trying not to feel a bit defensive.

"Julia! Hurry and eat. I want you to play baseball with me." Hank sat nearby, his cheeks bulging with food as he wolfed down his meal.

Whew! Julia was thankful for the interruption.

"Henry David Hostetler! *Sei net so rilpsich,*" his mother reprimanded him in a stern voice. "You should swallow your food before speaking."

Looking ashamed, Hank instantly swallowed with a big gulp. He then leaned one elbow on the table and looked dejectedly at his plate, no longer interested in eating. Julia had never seen the boy look so forlorn.

"What did your *mudder* say to him?" Julia whispered to Martin.

He chuckled softly. "She told him not to be rude."

Julia's heart wrenched. "But he looks so sad now."

"Then hurry with your meal and we won't disappoint him," Martin said.

Avoiding Marva's steady gaze, she ate quickly. Soon, she laid her fork down and took a last swallow of water. "I'm done. Shall we play baseball?"

Hank popped out of his chair like a jack-in-the-box and came to take her good hand.

"*Ja! Komm* on," he cried.

As she turned, she saw that a game had already started in the fallow hayfield. They didn't wait for Martin to untangle his long legs from beneath the table as they hurried toward the baseball diamond. Julia tossed him a glance over her shoulder, knowing he was following behind, laughing and shaking his head.

Right then, she decided that she loved work frolics with the Amish. In fact, there were a lot of things she loved about these people.

"Run, Julia! Run!" thirteen-year-old Alice Schwartz yelled.

"*Ja*, run, Julia," Hank chimed in.

Martin had hit the ball for her and she sprinted toward first base. Even with the extra encouragement, she wasn't fast enough. James Yoder, one of the bishop's teenage sons, tagged her out.

Martin frowned, thinking he should have assigned himself to first base and had someone else hit for Julia. He would have ensured that she made it in safe. For some reason, he felt protective of her.

Like always, she took the out good-naturedly. He was impressed by what a good sport she was.

"You're too fast for me, James," she said with a breathless laugh. "Next time, I'll ask Martin to knock it to the other side of the field."

James just smiled shyly. Julia returned to the dusty area on the outskirts of Bishop Yoder's hayfield that had been designated as the "out" area.

"That's okay, Julia. I get tagged out all the time. I'm never fast enough either," Hank said.

Martin watched the two as they laughed and chatted together. Hank was like a younger brother to her.

Too bad her mother hadn't joined them today. Martin was sure that, if Sharon would simply soften her heart, she would enjoy being with them, too. Over the past few weeks since he'd known them, he'd observed that Sharon had no friends. She didn't do anything but work and rest when she got too tired. That wasn't much of a life. And even though he'd been as kind to the woman as possible, he didn't know how to get through to her. Julia was all light, fun and joy. But Sharon seemed the complete opposite—dark, morose and sad. He knew something was holding her back from becoming friends with the Amish. Something big. Why did she dislike his people so much?

The next batter got another out, so they changed sides. Now Julia became the first baseman.

Little Hannah Yoder, the bishop's six-year-old daughter, came up to bat. The child looked tiny standing there, her legs and arms so thin as she lifted the heavy bat.

"Pitch softly," Martin called to Jakob Fisher, who was the pitcher.

Jakob nodded and tossed the ball ever so gently, ensuring the girl got a hit. Pressing her tongue to her upper lip, Hannah swung hard, knocking the ball just a few yards away.

"Run, Hannah! Run!" the other children yelled. Martin noticed that Julia screamed encouragement, in spite of being on the opposing team.

Hannah took off at a sprint, running as fast as she could go. As she approached first base, her long skirts tangled around her legs. She fell, reaching her arms toward the base and skidding in the dirt.

"Oh, Hannah!" Julia cringed.

"Safe!" one of the boys called, waving his arms over top of the sprawled girl.

Hannah promptly pulled one knee up against her chest and burst into tears. Martin watched as Julia scooped the child into her arms to comfort her. She held her injured hand away, using the strength of her forearm to cuddle the child.

"There, there, sweetums. Let me see. Where are you hurt?" Julia spoke in a sympathetic voice.

Martin hurried to the base, accompanied by the other players. As they crowded around, Hannah continued to cry.

Julia drew back enough to see the injury. The child's black tights had been shredded across the knee, her skin bloodied by the small abrasion. Thankfully, it didn't look too serious.

"I got hurt," Hannah cried as giant tears rolled down her cheeks.

"I know, *boppli*," Julia cooed. "But I think you'll be okay. We need to clean this up and put a bandage on it. You're so brave." Julia looked up, searching the crowd of faces until she saw Martin. "Can you carry her to the house?"

He nodded, his heart swelling with joy that she had sought him out.

"Of course. *Komm* to me, Hannah." Copying Julia's sympathetic voice, he reached for the child. Still crying, Hannah thrust out her arms and clung tightly to his neck as he carried her across the field.

A trail of children followed.

"Is she all right?" Hank asked, trotting along beside him.

"*Ja*, she'll be fine." Julia looked into Hannah's eyes and smiled. "Won't you, *boppli*?"

Hannah nodded, her little chin quivering as she tucked her face against Martin's chest.

The moment Sarah Yoder saw her daughter was hurt, she came running.

"What happened?" she cried.

Julia quickly explained, trying to lighten the moment. "But she made it safe to first base."

"She did, huh? That's *gut*!" Sarah seemed surprised as she examined the wound.

"*Ja*, she ran really hard," Hank said.

"*Ach*, that's my girl. Now, let's get you inside." Sarah took the girl into her own arms and headed toward the back door to the kitchen.

Julia went with them but Martin blocked the way so the other kids wouldn't follow.

"Hannah is going to be okay. Go on back to your game now," he told them.

They did as asked and Martin entered the house. He found Julia seated at the table. Hannah was perched on the kitchen table with Julia rubbing her back in a circular motion. Sarah was searching the cupboards and soon pulled out some antiseptic and little bandages.

Within moments, the ruined tights had been removed and the wound cleansed. When Sarah reached for the bandage, Hannah hugged tight against Julia.

"I want Julia to do it," Hannah said.

"That would be fine," Sarah said, handing over the bandage.

Smiling as if she had been awarded a great honor, Julia pulled the sticky strips off and put the bandage on the wound, pressing it down with a gentle touch.

"There! That didn't hurt too much, did it? You're almost good as new," she said.

Hannah looked at her knee and smiled, showing a tooth missing in front. "*Danke*, Julia."

"*Gaern gscheh, boppli.*" With one last hug, Julia set the girl on her own two feet.

Once again, Martin couldn't believe how good Julia's Deitsch was getting or how sweet she was with children. Without a doubt, he knew Julia would make a wonderful mother.

"Would you like some ice cream? Your *vadder* churned it especially for the frolic," Sarah told Hannah.

The girl nodded and took her mother's hand. The two walked outside together.

"That was nice," Martin said.

Julia nodded. She didn't speak for a few moments. Her eyes shimmered with moisture as she stared after the child.

"You know, I was so sad when Mom and I first moved here to Colorado," she finally said. "I felt lost and afraid. But now, I feel so happy inside. So calm and peaceful. And I know it has to do with all that I've been learning about God. I feel closer to Him than ever before. It also has to do with you and the new Amish friends I've made. Because of you, I don't feel alone anymore."

He stared at her, fascinated by the way her hair glimmered in the fading sunlight. "That's nice. I'm glad you feel that way. I liked how you cared for little Hannah."

"She's a sweet girl. I felt so bad that she fell down."

He grunted. "You're very nurturing."

She laughed. "That's not a characteristic I would use to describe myself. I always thought I was a bit rough, not nurturing at all. But with both my parents' illnesses, I've learned a lot."

He shrugged. "We are always changing, growing and

learning. Certain situations bring out different sides to our personalities that sometimes surprise us. My *gross-mammi* used to say the older we become, the more we become the person we really are inside."

"Grossmammi?"

"Grandmother," he supplied.

"That's a nice saying. I like it," she said. "It's probably true. I used to think I was weak and dependent upon my parents. Maybe that's why I clung to Dallin so much."

"Dallin?"

"My ex-fiancé. He dumped me so he could marry my best friend, Debbie. He lied and stole from me, too."

"Ah, that wasn't very kind," he said.

"No, it wasn't. I was afraid of being alone. But after my father died, I learned to be strong and independent. My mother depends on me and I can't let her down. I promised him I'd always take care of her," she said.

"One of the Ten Commandments is to honor your father and mother. Sharon is blessed to have a dutiful daughter like you," he said.

She laughed off his words. "Well, I don't know about that."

He stepped closer and she looked up at him. For several moments, he felt mesmerized as he gazed into her beautiful eyes.

"Julia, would you *komm* with me, please? There's something I want to show you before the daylight is gone."

He held out his hand. Without speaking, she reached over and enfolded his fingers with hers. The warmth of her touch sent currents of energy pulsing up his arm. He led her out the back way, skirting around the house so they wouldn't be seen. In silence, he harnessed his horse to the buggy and they drove away.

"Will we be missed?" she asked as the horse settled into a quick trot.

"My *vadder* will know not to worry about us," he said.

She chuckled. "I doubt that will provide any solace for Hank when he discovers we're gone."

"*Ja*, he is crazy about you. He tells everyone that you are his girl," Martin said.

She smiled at that and they rode for a time in silence.

"Where are you taking me?" she asked once they were a mile down the road.

"You will see."

Within minutes, they arrived at their destination and Martin pulled the buggy off the side of the road. The dusky sky allowed just enough light for them to see before the sun faded behind the Wet Mountains to the west. With the Sangre de Cristo Mountains in the east as a backdrop, the vast fields before them showed nothing but drab brown.

"In the summer, this will all be green with growth," he said.

"Where are we?" she asked, huddling within her coat and shivering.

He reached into the back and grabbed the warm quilt he kept there before spreading it over her legs. "This is my place. My farm."

He tried to prevent a note of *hochmut* from entering his voice. *Hochmut* was the arrogant pride of the world and something he should shun.

She nodded, gazing at the barren land with curiosity. Without looking, he knew it was dotted by a few boulders and scrubby trees that he would remove once he set the plow to the fields. But just now, he could hardly take his eyes off Julia, eager to see her response.

"It's lovely. I can see why you bought this land. It's close to town and filled with promise," she said.

He exhaled, realizing he'd been holding his breath. For some reason, he wanted her approval more than anything. "I'm glad you like it. I've got sixty-five acres with good water rights. I'm going to grow barley, oats and hay. It may not look like much right now, but one day, this land will all be fenced off. The rocks and boulders will be removed and the fields will be full of life."

"It'll take a lot of hard work but I know you're up to the task," she said.

He nodded and pointed to the east. "Over there, I'll build a fine barn like my *vadder*'s. And over there, I'll plow the ground for a vegetable garden." He pointed to the west. "Over here, I'll build a fine house for my *fraa*. I'll put up a clothes line for the laundry and build flower beds and a nice lawn for my *kinder* to play on."

She stared, her eyes unblinking as she took in his every word. "I imagine you'll want a chicken coop, too."

He laughed and nodded. She seemed so intuitive. "*Ja*, my *familye* will need plenty of eggs and chickens to eat."

"Have you ever killed a chicken?" she asked, her eyes crinkled with repulsion.

"*Ja*, many times. Does that upset you?" Oh, how he hoped she wasn't squeamish about such things. After all, the Amish raised what they ate. It was the way things were on a farm.

"*Ne*, I've cooked meat many times. It doesn't bother me as long as I don't have to kill it myself."

"Then I would do it for you," he promised.

She frowned and looked away. It was then he realized what he'd just said. He hoped she didn't assume he was proposing marriage. Because he wasn't. She was *Englisch*. They could never wed.

"Jules, I... I didn't mean that you and I would, that we would—"

She held up a hand to stop him. "I know what you meant. It's all right."

She was quiet then, as if absorbed in her own thoughts. He gave her some space, letting her think. Then, he decided to confess something to her.

"I've almost given up hope of ever marrying but I have faith *Gott* has a plan for me. It's just that you're so easy to talk to, Jules. And sometimes, I feel as if I can confide anything to you. It's like I've known you all my life. But in my heart of hearts, I know we can never be anything more than friends," he said.

There. He'd spoken what was in his heart. The next step would have to come from her. She would need to decide what she wanted in life and whether she would convert or remain *Englisch*.

"If I were to convert and marry an Amish man, would my husband let me keep my soap store and continue selling my products?" she asked.

Hmm. He blinked. Interesting how she'd asked that question. "I cannot speak for all Amish men, but I certainly would allow it. I wouldn't tell my wife what she could and could not do."

"I'm glad you're not like that," she said.

He heaved a deep sigh. "I've heard that some Amish men are cruel and domineering, though I know Bishop Yoder would never tolerate such abuse within our *Gmay*. He'd put a stop to it quick."

She smiled. "Yes, knowing the bishop as well as I do, I don't believe he would allow such things to go on. And I can't imagine him dominating Sarah."

Martin laughed at the thought. "Many of our *weibsleit*, including my own *mamm*, make crafts to sell in town. Baked goods, cheese, rag rugs, furniture, you name it. It helps supplement their *familye* incomes."

She nodded, deep in thought.

"I believe both spouses should be in their marriage by choice and not because they are forced," he said. "I would rather lead my *familye* to do what is right with love and kind persuasion, not with an iron fist."

"That is *gut*. I'm happy to hear that," she said.

They didn't speak again for several moments and he hoped he'd said the right things. But deep inside, he meant every word. He didn't know what to expect. For Julia to fall into his arms and ask to be baptized immediately? No, of course not. Her life wasn't that simple. After all, she had her mother to think about. Converting to the Amish faith was a huge and complicated commitment. Her first obligation was to her mother.

As night closed in on them, he drove her home in silence. And when they arrived, they found her mother standing on the front porch, waiting for them. She had a heavy shawl wrapped around her shoulders, her face creased with concern.

Martin helped Julia out of the buggy. "*Danke* for going with me tonight."

"And *danke* for a *wundervoll* evening." Her voice sounded whisper soft.

He nodded, hardly able to speak. As she turned and hurried to her mother, his throat felt tight and he couldn't swallow.

"Hi, Mom. Oh, how I missed you. I wish you could have gone with us." She embraced Sharon in a tight hug.

"It's late and I was worried," Sharon said, her voice trembling.

Martin wondered if she'd been crying. He hoped not.

Together, the two women went inside and Martin couldn't hear the rest of their conversation. As she closed the door, Julia glanced back at him and waved.

Martin climbed into the buggy and headed home. As he drove through the cold night air, his chest ached. He would never ask Julia to go against her mother. He could see that they loved each other and it wouldn't be right. His faith taught him that a child must honor their parents. And because he would never leave his faith, that meant he and Julia could never marry.

They would never be anything more than friends and that hurt most of all.

Chapter Ten

The electrician came the following Wednesday. It was the morning before Thanksgiving and he worked all day installing a new fuse box on the outside of the house and running new wires to the attic. He brought the entire system up to code. Other than that, Julia had no idea what he was doing. When he finished, he smiled wide as he flipped on the kitchen light switch and they had power.

Mom was elated but Julia felt a heaviness inside that she couldn't explain. Not only did the repair bill cost a lot of money but it was as if she were betraying all that Martin had taught her about being humble. As if she had just let the world inside her home.

Thankfully, Martin wasn't here to see what was going on. Because she was *Englisch*, Julia knew he wouldn't say a word about her having electricity in her home but she knew he wouldn't approve. And no matter how hard Mom encouraged her to do so, Julia couldn't bring herself to use the electrical switches or appliances such as hand mixers, toasters and can openers.

She'd attended church with Martin again. During the many times they'd been alone together, she'd asked him lots of questions about his faith and he'd patiently answered every one. Coupled with her personal prayer and study of the Scriptures, his responses seemed so logical and she liked what she heard. In spite of her mother's resistance, Julia felt a sense of calm as she listened to Martin's explanations and it only made her hunger for more.

Thanksgiving was a lonely affair. More than ever, Julia missed the warm camaraderie of a loving family and friends. But most of all, she missed Martin.

Mom made a roast turkey breast with mashed potatoes, gravy and rolls. Julia made pumpkin pie with whipped cream. Sitting alone together in their quiet apartment, they didn't talk much and Julia picked at her food.

"You're not hungry?" Sharon asked.

"Not much but everything is delicious," Julia said.

She couldn't help wishing they had accepted Linda Hostetler's invitation to join Martin's family for their feast. But Mom wouldn't hear of it.

"Mom?"

"Hmm?" Sharon didn't look up as she scooped a spoonful of cranberry sauce onto her plate.

"What would you think if I decided to become Amish?"

Mom's fork clattered to her plate and her mouth dropped open with shock. "You're not serious."

Julia swallowed hard. "I've been thinking about it."

Mom stood and scooted back her chair so hard that it toppled to the floor. With stiff, angry movements, she set it back up, then grabbed up her plate and stormed over to the kitchen sink.

"I can't believe you would even consider such a thing. The Amish? Really, Julia!"

She watched her mother for several moments, trying to gather her courage. After all, she was a fully grown woman who worked hard and paid the bills. She should be able to make choices for herself.

"I don't know why you're so against them," she said. "They're kind, hardworking and devout. I love their faith. It's come to mean a great deal to me."

Mom turned to look at her, holding the dish cloth in one hand. "Yes, and if you choose such a life, you'll forfeit all your freedoms. You'll be controlled by whatever whim your husband and the church elders might force upon you."

Julia just stared. Dallin had been so manipulative and domineering that freedom of choice was extremely important to her. But she and Martin had discussed this issue and she didn't believe he would treat his wife that way. She longed for a family of her own. Loved ones she could care about and shower her love upon. She'd thought she was going to have that with Dallin. But Mom's accusations sounded so authentic. What if Julia was wrong? What if Martin wasn't as he seemed?

"I've never seen any of the Amish men treat their wives like that. Why do you think that's the way they act?" she asked.

"When I was a girl, I saw Amish men treating their wives and daughters quite poorly. They're careful and quiet about it but it's still there, hidden behind the walls of their homes where outsiders can't see in," Mom said.

"Martin isn't like that. He would never treat me that way," Julia said.

Or would he? She didn't think so, but she hadn't known him very long.

"Has he…has he asked you to marry him?" Mom asked, her voice filled with fear.

"No, he wouldn't do that. Not as long as I'm *Englisch*. We're just friends." And yet, she wished they could take their relationship to a more romantic level. But that couldn't happen as long as she wasn't Amish. And she couldn't convert as long as her mother disapproved. So they were at a standstill.

Mom nodded, her eyes shimmering with tears. "Has he asked you to convert?"

Julia shook her head. "He wouldn't ask me to do that either. Not as long as he thinks I'd be going against your wishes. He wants me to decide for myself. You see? You're wrong about him. He only wants my happiness and what is best for me."

Though she said the words, Julia wasn't sure they were true. Was Martin really as wonderful as he seemed? How could she ever know for sure?

Mom turned and made a pretense of washing dishes but Julia could see she was upset. She stood and went to her mother, touching her shoulder.

"Mom, what is it? What's wrong?" she asked.

Mom whirled around and hugged her fiercely. "I… I'm just so afraid I'm going to lose you to those people."

"Those people? You talk about them as if they're monsters. And they're not."

"But they don't like the *Englisch*. They won't let you come see me very often, if at all."

"No, Mama," Julia soothed. "You'll never lose me as long as I live. Put your fears at ease. I won't let anyone or anything come between us. I promise you that."

And Julia meant it. As long as she had breath in her body, she would look after her mother. She'd given her word to her father. She would never become Amish if it meant turning her back on her mother.

They stood there for some time, until Julia felt her mother's body stop trembling. Then they washed the dishes together and retired to the living room where they took turns reading out loud from an Agatha Christie novel. Later that afternoon, they napped and relaxed and spoke no more about the Amish. That evening, Julia found some solace in the Scriptures. But in her heart, she felt no peace. She missed Martin more than she could say and longed to be with him. And she realized that, whether she liked it or not, her feelings for him had grown.

The next day, they received their first snowfall. As Julia stared out the chilled windowpane in her bedroom, she felt mesmerized by the gently drifting flakes that soon increased and blanketed the ground in pristine white. Kansas had snow but not like this. In the night, the temperature took a dive and she was more than grateful Martin had repaired their roof and secured the firewood they needed.

She couldn't help thinking about the night of the frolic when Martin had taken her to see his farmland. As she'd listened to him describe his plans to build a barn and a fine house to live in, she'd caught his excitement and longed to be a part of his dreams. Though he hadn't proposed to her, she'd caught the gist of the moment. If she were to convert to the Amish faith, he would pursue her.

When she'd moved to Colorado, she hadn't planned to fall in love but she had. With Martin and with his Amish people. To all appearances, they were just friends. But in Julia's heart, he meant much more to her. The love she felt for him was different from what she'd felt for

Dallin. It was sweet and pure and made her realize they could never wed.

As Julia got ready for the day, a feeling of dread and anticipation thrummed through her veins. Today, she would have the bandages on her hand removed and make her first batch of soap. Martin had promised to come into town that afternoon to help. And the thought of seeing him again made her fizzy with happiness.

Though she tried to fight off the feeling, she couldn't wait to see him. But being near him only prolonged the torture. His work for her was almost finished. Her relationship with God had grown and her belief in the Amish faith was strong.

But she couldn't defy her mother by converting. Which meant she had to put a stop to their interaction. After today, she might bump into him or one of his people on the street, but nothing more. And that thought made her want to cry.

"Have you asked her to convert?" Bishop Yoder asked.

It was midmorning and Martin sat in the bishop's home, having come to seek his advice. It was the day after Thanksgiving and Martin was on his way into town, to help Julia make soap.

"Maybe she just needs a little incentive," the bishop said.

Martin leaned back on the old sofa and crossed his arms. The black woodstove nearby provided plenty of warmth. Even so, he still felt a chill run up his spine. He would love nothing more than to ask Julia to be baptized but he couldn't do that. She had to make this decision on her own.

"Honestly, I fear her answer," Martin said. "Her *mudder* is ailing and doesn't approve of the Amish. I'm afraid Julia would choose her *mamm* over conversion to our faith."

The bishop's eyes were filled with compassion and wisdom. "*Ja*, she is hardworking and devoted to her *mudder*. That is *gut*. You wouldn't want her if she were the type of woman who would desert her *mamm*. If she would convert, she would make a good *fraa* for you."

Martin stared, thunderstruck by his feelings. He cared deeply for Julia. He loved her. It was that simple. But because she wasn't Amish, he could never think of her as anything but a friend. So, what could he do?

"She doesn't need to abandon her *mudder* in order to convert to our faith. She can still visit and care for her *mamm*. Perhaps she doesn't know that. You might want to tell her," the bishop said.

Martin tilted his head. "I appreciate you saying so but I think she knows. The problem is bigger than that. She was engaged to be married once before and her fiancé treated her rather badly. Also, I don't think Julia will convert without her *mamm*'s blessing. Sharon is so against the Amish faith and I don't believe Julia will defy her *mudder* even if she has the conviction that it's right."

"*Ach*, I see. She seeks to honor her *mudder* just as you would honor your *eldre*. This is a difficult dilemma. I don't know what you want me to tell you, *sohn*," the bishop said.

"I'm not sure either," Martin said.

Bishop Yoder leaned forward in his chair and rested his elbows on his knees. His gaze drilled into Martin's with a steely edge. "If she will convert and agree to live by the *Ordnung*, I would be happy to baptize her.

Perhaps after that, the two of you might wish to marry. We shall see."

Yes, they would have to wait and see.

"But I must warn you, Martin. Don't let your feelings for Julia draw you over to the *Englisch* world. A lot is at stake here. But you already know what you must do if she won't convert."

Yes, Martin knew only too well. He must turn and walk away and never look back. If she wouldn't join his faith, it would be too dangerous to remain friends. It might give the wrong impression to his people and it could lead to other dangerous things. To abandon his Amish faith was tantamount to turning his back on his eternal salvation. He'd be shunned by his people. He'd lose everything that meant anything to him. His *familye* and friends. His home. His sense of belonging.

His *Gott*.

And he couldn't do that no matter how much he cared for Julia.

The bishop sat back, having said his piece. Martin nodded and came to his feet. He knew what he must do. Knew that he must be strong. If Julia chose not to join his Amish faith, he must let her go.

Chapter Eleven

By early afternoon, Julia was in her workroom, ready to make soap. She lifted a heavy stainless steel stockpot off the shelf and carried it to the work counter. Using the strength of her arms to support the pan, she avoided straining her left hand. The doctor had just removed the bandages and pronounced her wounds completely healed, though her muscles had atrophied from lack of use and would take time to build up their strength again.

After measuring out some of the oils, she picked up the pan to move it over to the stovetop. She lost her grip on one handle and felt the pot falling. But suddenly, a pair of large hands reached to take the brunt of its weight.

She whirled around in surprise. "Martin!"

He must have just arrived. He'd promised to come help her make her first batch of soap today and she admitted silently to herself that she was delighted to see him.

"*Ach*, you shouldn't be lifting heavy things yet. What did the doctor say about your hand?" He showed a dubious frown as he set the pan on the stove. He then removed his winter coat and black felt hat and set them aside on a chair.

"It's fine with minimal scarring." She almost flinched when he reached for her left hand and took it softly into his.

The pads of his fingertips felt rough as he caressed her fingers. He turned her hand as he eyed the new skin. His touch was infinitely gentle and she felt currents of excitement pulsing up her arm.

"Look! My left hand is smaller than my right." Giving a jittery laugh, she pulled free of his grasp and held up both hands, which showed a slight disparity in the size of the two.

Martin nodded. "*Ja*, I saw this happen when Jeremiah Beiler broke his leg. But don't fear. Within a couple of weeks, you won't even notice that your left hand was ever injured."

His reassurance gave her the courage to maintain a positive attitude. She peered behind him for some sign of his brother. "Hank isn't with you today?"

"*Ne*, he has a bad head cold. *Mamm* made him stay at home. She didn't want him out in the chilled air."

She frowned, feeling doubtful. "I'll bet he wasn't happy about that."

Martin flashed a smile that didn't quite reach his eyes. "You are right. He wasn't happy at all when I left this morning."

"Well, be sure to tell him I missed him," she said.

Not wanting him to see her sad expression, she turned to face the stockpot. After all, today was their last day to work together in the soap studio. Though she would never admit it out loud, it was a melancholy time for Julia. There'd be no more detailed discussions about the

Amish beliefs. No more frolics or tulips from Hank or thrilling buggy rides.

And no more Martin.

He glanced around the tidy workroom. "Where is Sharon today?"

Julia shrugged. "Like Hank, she isn't feeling well. She's upstairs resting."

"Then it's just us two?" he asked.

She nodded, not trusting her clogged voice.

"Then we can practice your Deitsch. *Weller daag iss heit?*" he asked suddenly.

She blinked, surprised that she understood most of his question. He had asked her what day it was.

"It is *Freidawk*, the day after Thanksgiving," she said, indicating it was Friday.

To distract herself, she reached for a jug of olive oil and slowly measured it into the pot. She jerked when he reached to help her, taking the bulk of the weight in his two strong hands.

"*Gut.* Now, can you repeat my question back to me?" he asked, setting the empty bottle aside.

"Sure! *Weller dog iss heit?*"

He promptly burst into laughter.

Without thinking, she buffeted his shoulder in a playful gesture. "What? Did I say it wrong?"

"You did. You just asked me what dog is it."

She laughed, too, wondering why she was trying so hard to learn his language. After all, she wouldn't see him anymore and speaking Deitsch wouldn't be fun without him. But then she reminded herself that she still wanted to be able to talk to his people when they came into her store. For a few brief moments, she thought about asking him to continue giving her lessons a couple evenings each week. But no. That would only invite trouble.

He went suddenly very still, his gaze trained toward the hallway. Julia caught a movement out of her peripheral vision and turned to find her mom standing in the threshold leading to the back rooms. She must have heard their laughter because her scowl looked dark and deep.

"Are you almost finished?" Sharon asked, her voice stern.

"No, Mom. We've only just started the first batch," Julia said.

"Well, I'll be upstairs if you need me." Sharon's eyes narrowed on Martin and Julia knew the comment was for him, to let him know she was nearby.

Before Julia could say anything else, Mom turned on her heels and climbed the stairs to their apartment above.

Julia faced Martin again, feeling a tad embarrassed by her mother's actions. "I... I'm sorry about that. She really is feeling under the weather today."

He nodded. "*Ach*, there's no harm done. Now, what do you need me to do?"

She stepped over to the work counter. Except for the heavy buckets, she'd already set out the various ingredients they would need.

Seeing Martin's curious glance, she pointed at a bowl of grayish powder. "This is colloidal oatmeal. Today, we'll be making two super batches of oatmeal, milk and honey soap."

He tilted his head to one side. "Super batches?"

"*Ja*, super batching is when you make four or more batches of soap at one time. I'll need to make dozens of super batches in order to fill all my orders by the end of January."

He grunted. "That's a lot of soap."

"*Ja*, and it will take time to make it and then four to five weeks for it to dry and cure. My oatmeal soap smells delicious and should sell well during the month of February."

He blinked. "It sounds good enough to eat."

She nodded and rested her fingertips against a stainless steel pitcher of goat milk, which she'd acquired from Martin's mother. "Except for the lye, you could definitely eat my soap. It's made of all-natural ingredients that most people cook with on a daily basis. Olive oil, coconut oil, palm oil... It lathers beautifully and is nourishing to the skin. And it doesn't dry you out like manufactured soap does."

"Why is that?"

"The manufactured soap is filled with chemicals I can't even pronounce," she said.

He chuckled. "All right, you're the expert. What should I do?"

He rolled up the long sleeves of his shirt, ready to work. For a moment, she gazed at his muscular arms, wishing things could be different between them. Wishing they could...

She shook her head and walked over to the heavy-duty shelves he'd built for her and reached for a large bottle of canola oil. Before she could lift it, he picked it up with very little effort.

She pointed and he set it on the counter beside the stove. After popping off the lid, she measured out what she needed, turned the stove burner onto low and pointed to the next ingredient. Working together, Martin lifted the heavy containers while she measured everything out. Soon, she had the oils melting inside the stockpot and turned her attention to the distilled water and lye.

Handing Martin a face mask, a pair of goggles and some rubber gloves, she indicated that he should put them on. She did likewise, laughing at how funny they both looked. She wished she had a camera but knew the Amish didn't take pictures because they didn't believe in making graven images of themselves. But she didn't need a picture. As long as she lived, she would hold this memory in her mind.

With careful precision, she poured the lye into the distilled water. Martin reached for a plastic spoon to stir the mixture with.

"It's nice that you and my *mudder* have so much in common," he said.

She agreed. In many ways, she felt closer to Linda than she did her own mother. Linda was so accepting of Julia, while Sharon insisted on rejecting Martin and anything to do with the Amish. Under the circumstances, it would be difficult to stay friends with Linda but Julia hoped they could.

He watched earnestly as she stirred the lye water. It immediately turned cloudy, then went crystal clear after a few minutes.

Using a battery-operated thermometer gun, she measured the temperature of the lye and the oils. She rested the palm of her hand against the outside of the metal pitcher.

"Touch here," she said. "You can feel the heat of the lye. The moment you add it to the water, it can race up to a temperature of two hundred degrees."

He felt the container and his eyes widened. "*Ja*, it is very hot."

"While we make soap, we must remember that we have become scientists and we're working with some volatile chemicals. We always want to be careful not to make mistakes." She stepped over to the stove and gave the oils a quick stir, checking to ensure it didn't scorch.

"I always loved science when I was in school," he said.

"Well, even though you only go to the eighth grade, you can still learn things just by working and living life," she said.

He nodded. "You do understand us, don't you? I've never really felt like I quit school. On the farm, I learn something new every day."

His expression was filled with curiosity as she measured out the fragrance oils and micas to color the soap.

His nose twitched. "That smells *gut*."

Thinking the same thing, she reached for the goat milk and poured it into the oil mixture. After blending, she added the ground oatmeal and honey. He stood near, leaning over her to watch. She felt his warm breath touch her cheek. He smelled of horses and peppermint. His presence so close beside her made her highly aware of him as an attractive man and her hands shook slightly.

"Do you need me to stir that for you?" he asked quietly.

She shook her head, embarrassed that he had noticed her nervousness.

Working fast, she poured the lye mixture into the oils and used a battery-powered stick blender and long, oversize plastic spoon to mix it to a thin trace. Then she divided the batter into other containers and added the colored micas. Martin watched with wide eyes as she then did an in-the-pot swirl of white, light shimmery gold and a darker gold color. The brilliance of the micas seemed perfect for this creamy soap as they swirled together.

"Those colors are beautiful. *Mamm* always makes our soap plain white," he said.

"The secret is to not overmix or you'll lose the design. It's now ready to pour into the block molds." She nodded at the huge molds she had already set on a wooden rolling dolly and prepped with freezer paper and Mylar liners.

"Can you lift and pour it for me?" she asked.

He nodded, clasped the handles of the stockpot and poured the mixture evenly into the two big molds. What was normally a heavy, challenging chore for Julia seemed like a simple task to a man of his strength.

"Someday, I'd like to buy a pot tipper. You just use a lever to pour the batter into the molds," she said.

She used a flat spatula to scrape down the sides of the pot, getting every drop of soap into the molds. Then, she lifted one mold and tamped it to get all the air bubbles out of the soap. With her weak hand, her actions weren't very effective.

"Here, let me do that." He brushed her aside so he could lift each mold onto the solid floor where he smacked them gently several times.

"How much soap does each mold hold?" he asked as he set the soap back on the cart.

"Twenty-five pounds. I'll get 172 squares of nice, fat bars that fit well in a person's hand and don't dissolve as quickly as a thin bar."

He took a little inhale, his face mask sucking inward.

"That's a lot of soap. I don't think *Mamm* has ever made that much for our *familye*."

"*Ja*, but your *mamm* doesn't sell her soap. She just makes it for your own use."

He removed his face mask and took another deep inhale. "Mmm, the soap sure smells *gut*."

"Yes, it does." She couldn't help feeling pleased that he liked the fragrance. She had invented this soap on her own and was rather pleased with the results.

Sliding the dolly over to the far wall where it wouldn't be disturbed, she covered the molds with a sheet of cardboard she'd saved and then wrapped it all with an old, tattered quilt.

"Why do you wrap it up like that? Are you afraid the hot soap might get cold?" He chuckled at his own humor.

She laughed, too. "I know it seems odd but I want the soap to go through a gel phase where it will get very hot. The result is that the colors brighten and look beautiful after we cut it into squares tomorrow."

"Ahh, I see. Do you need me to *komm* help you cut the soap?"

She hesitated. Seeing him again in the morning would be wonderful but she couldn't. She'd already told Mom that this was his last day of work. For her own sanity, she didn't dare see him again either.

"*Ne*, I think Mom and I can manage all right. I will also make a super batch of lavender soap and one of orange calendula. On Monday, I'll make a super batch of apple sage and one of black raspberry."

He frowned. "Are you coming to church with me on the next Church Sunday?"

She froze. For a few moments, she'd forgotten that she planned to stay away from the Amish. She thought about going to church with him again but knew it was foolhardy. It would only confuse their families and his *Gmay*. It would be better if she went to the Christian church here in town, though she knew it wouldn't be the same. Something about the Amish doctrine really spoke to her heart. Something she couldn't deny. Yet, it also brought her mother's disapproval. Julia's relationship with God had become so strong and she wasn't willing to give that up.

"We'll see. Can I let you know when we get closer to Sunday?" she asked.

He nodded but didn't meet her eyes. "Of course. Whatever you like. I'll check with you again next week."

Julia turned away, trying not to be afraid that she was losing him.

Martin didn't try to persuade Julia to join him at church. He was struggling to remember that it was her choice. But he'd be sure to stop by her store next Saturday to invite her again and see if he could give her a ride.

They worked in companionable silence, making another super batch. At lunchtime, they shared some sandwiches and fruit. The afternoon passed quickly and it was soon time for him to leave.

Julia stepped over to the chair and picked up his hat and coat, handing them to him. As she walked with him to the front door, she whisked an envelope from off the counter beside the cash register and held it out to him.

"This is for you," she said, not looking at him.

He took it but didn't open it. He already knew what was inside. His final paycheck.

"Is there nothing else I can do for you? I... I don't

need to get paid. I can help you just because we're friends," he said.

How he wished she could come up with a long list of chores for him to do. How he wished he could stay here with her forever.

"There's nothing else left to do except work my soap store. You've done wonders and I'm so grateful." She turned and looked around the room. Everything was tidy and in its place. Cheery and inviting. A delightful store for customers to shop in.

She walked to the door and opened it. She even stepped outside with him onto the front porch. He gazed out at the skiff of snow that was just starting to fall. It was dark already and he wondered where the day had gone. He should be getting home.

She shivered against the frigid air and folded her arms. He didn't think before he swung his warm coat around her shoulders. As he held it closed just beneath her chin, he stepped nearer. Their gazes clashed, then locked. He felt lost, drowning in the beauty of her face. Before he thought to stop himself, he ducked his head down and kissed her gently, so softly that it felt like the brush of a butterfly against his lips. She gave a little sigh, telling him she felt the connection between them, too.

"Jules, I wish things could be different. I wish—"

The rattle of the door caused them to jerk apart. Julia gasped in dismay.

Looking up, Martin saw Sharon standing in the threshold, a prudish look on her face.

"The snow is getting worse and the roads will be icy. It's time for you to leave, Martin." Sharon spoke in a stern voice as she folded her arms.

"Um, *ja*, you are right. *Gut nacht*, Jules," he said.

"Goodbye, Martin." Julia held out his coat to him.

Their fingers touched briefly as he took it from her and quickly put it on. He nodded to her, trying to offer his silent support, yet feeling confused and mortified and even a little angry at the situation. Why did Sharon have to be so hard-hearted? Why couldn't she see that Julia belonged with the Amish?

He stepped back, closing his coat. As he did so, he caught Julia's light scent and couldn't help taking a deep breath.

Snowflakes stuck to his eyelashes and he blinked. Soon, the wet flakes would soak him clear through and he'd be cold on the ride home. If he didn't leave now, he never would.

He hurried over to his horse and buggy. As he climbed inside and closed the door, his thoughts were filled with turmoil. He gathered up the leather lead lines, forcing himself to go home.

The snow continued to fall as he pulled out of the parking lot. He gazed into his rearview mirror and stared back at the soapworks. Sharon went back inside but Julia stood right where he'd left her. He watched her until she faded from view.

Chapter Twelve

On December 1, Julia was up early. Though it was brisk outside, the morning blazed with sunlight. Perfect weather for the grand opening of Rose Soapworks and just in time for holiday shopping. She'd had some flyers and posters made and spread them around town several weeks earlier to advertise the event. She'd even put an ad in the local newspaper. Even so, she couldn't help feeling jittery inside. What if no one came? What if she was stuck with all this soap, lotions and other products she and Mom had worked so hard to make?

What if her new business flopped?

No! She mustn't think that way. Martin had taught her to have faith in God. She'd worked and prayed so hard, asking for help to make the store a success. Asking to know how to handle Mom's resistance to the Amish faith. She'd even attended the Christian church here in town but it wasn't the same as the Amish church. The message of Christ's atonement didn't sink as deeply into her heart as it did when she attended with the Amish. She'd only attended their church a couple of times but it had been enough. She'd felt the spirit of God in her heart and knew it was what she wanted in her life. And she missed the people she'd grown to love. Martin's *familye*, Bishop Yoder and even waspish old Marva Geingerich. She missed them all. And she realized that Martin had deepened the experience for her into a solid love of God and the Amish faith.

Determined to trust in the Lord, Julia pulled on her warm winter coat and carried the ladder outside. She had a large Grand Opening sign she wanted to hang across the front of the store before she opened the front door in twenty minutes.

"Martin!"

Bundled with a scarf and gloves, he stood leaning against the outer wall. Since she hadn't seen him for days, the shock of finding him here was even worse. A rush of joy, relief and dread washed over her all at once.

"What are you doing here?" she asked, dropping the unwieldy sign on the porch.

Pushing off the wall, he walked to her, a gentle smile curving his lips. That was how Martin was. Always calm, nonjudgmental and soothing.

"You mentioned last week you had a large sign you wanted to hang across your storefront. I figured you might need some help," he said.

His consideration touched her like nothing else could. "*Ja*, I do need help. Mom's back is in so much pain that she can hardly walk. The cold weather makes it worse."

He picked up the heavy sign. "Then let me help you."

He placed the sign in her hands, his touch so gentle, his gaze so inviting that she felt mesmerized. Without speaking, he showed her a heavy-duty staple gun he must have brought with him. Then he slid the ladder into position in front of the porch canopy. Stepping up on the rungs, he turned and reached toward her.

For a moment, Julia just stared. Then she moved into action and handed him one edge of the sign. He lifted it high, holding it in place with one hand. The crack of the staple gun filled the air as he affixed the sign to the canopy overhead. He then stepped down and moved the ladder over a bit. Julia held the weight of the sign up so it wouldn't sag and rip through the staples. Within minutes, Martin had the whole thing secured above the wooden porch and stepped down off the ladder.

The sign waved gently in the crisp morning breeze. The bright red lettering was so large that a person could see it way down at the other end of Main Street. Hopefully the townsfolk and ranchers' wives in the area would be curious and come check out her shop. But regardless of how her retail store did, she still had her soap contracts with KostSmart to depend upon.

Seeing the banner hanging across her storefront brought a welling of tears to her eyes. This moment meant so much to her. If Martin weren't here, she'd cry with happiness. Today, she would officially open her soapworks for business. Today was the culmination of so much effort. It was the outcome of a dream she'd had for years. And Martin had helped make it a reality.

"Oh, *danke*, Martin. *Danke* so much. I'm so glad you're here to share this moment with me," she exclaimed. Before she thought to stop herself, she gave him a quick hug.

He stepped back, blinking in surprise. "I... I... You're *willkomm*. I know how much this means to you."

"Can you stay for the opening of the store?" she asked.

"*Ne*, my *vadder* expects my help on the farm today. I have to leave now or he'll be worried."

Something about his manner made her believe his father didn't know he was here.

Carrying the staple gun, he stepped down off the porch. She stared after him, not wanting to let him go.

He gazed at her for several moments, as if he didn't want to leave either. "It was *gut* to see you, Jules."

She took a quick step toward him, wishing he could stay. "But when will I see you again?"

Oh, she shouldn't have said that. She'd been the one to push him away and now she was asking to see him again. She felt so confused. Her common sense told her that he must go, yet her heart wanted him to stay.

He hesitated. "My work is finished here. The bishop doesn't want me to *komm* into town unless I have business here."

"So, we can't be friends anymore," she said.

He looked reticent. "I… I'll *komm* again tomorrow morning. Now I must hurry. I hope you sell everything in your store. I know it will be a great success. Just have a little faith."

Watching him go, a fresh burst of tears filled her eyes. She nodded, biting her bottom lip. His encouragement meant everything to her.

Tomorrow! He'd come see her again in the morning.

Without another word, he turned and climbed into his buggy. As he directed the horse out of the parking lot, he lifted a hand in farewell. She waved, too, longing to run after him but knowing she must not.

Tomorrow! She'd see him again. The fears Dallin had instilled within her seemed to fade away. Martin would never hurt her the way Dallin had done. She could trust

Martin. She knew that now. But seeing him again was futile. It would only prolong the pain. Because nothing would change between them. Not as long as her mother disapproved of him and his religion.

Julia stood there until his buggy moved out of sight. Then she carried the ladder around to the back shed to put it away. Inside the store, she unlocked the front door. It wasn't opening time but she was ready for business. She gazed about the room. Everything looked so bright and cheery, like a Christmas wonderland filled with amazing secrets to explore. In each windowsill, battery-operated candles sat atop a bed of spun angel-hair glass. Hanging above them on green, shimmery ribbons was an assortment of red ornaments and white sparkly snowflakes. A pine cone wreath with red holly berries had been hung on the front door along with a little tinkling bell to alert her when someone came inside.

Quilted Christmas runners with cheery designs lined each tabletop where she showcased her handmade soaps, creams and lip balms. Garlands of tinsel hung from each display case. The air smelled sweet, a mixture of the fragrant soaps she'd made and the cinnamon and spice incense she'd set near the old mechanical cash register. Everything looked so jolly, yet Julia felt a leaden weight in her heart. If only Martin were still here, it would be a perfect day.

She'd see him tomorrow.

Clinging to that thought, Julia arranged a pile of dainty paper napkins beside the punch bowl. She and her mom had pulled out all the stops in decorating the store. With one exception: Julia had refused to put up a Christmas tree. Rather than tell her mom the Amish didn't have trees, she simply explained that she needed the room to display her soaps. Thankfully, Mom hadn't argued.

"I heard the front door. Was someone here?"

Sharon came into the room at that moment, carrying a platter of frosted Christmas cookies she'd baked the night before. She set them on a special table with a red cloth and the glass punch bowl. It wasn't every day that a new store opened in this sleepy town and they wanted to welcome their customers with refreshments. Because of the novelty of the store, Julia was certain every rancher and farmer's wife from miles around would step inside her door just to take a look. And since it was Christmas-time, they'd be searching for just the right gift.

"Um, I just unlocked the front door. But Martin was here. He stopped by to help me hang the Grand Opening sign. He just left." Julia wouldn't lie to her mom but turned away and fussed with a display of Christmas soaps, hoping to avoid another argument.

Mom didn't say a word as she poured red punch into the large bowl. Julia helped her, eager to hear the tinkling sound above their door ringing again and again.

She didn't have long to wait. They had just set out throwaway cups when the tinkling was followed by a group of Amish women wearing black traveling bonnets, heavy capes and black ankle boots.

"Linda! Lori! *Willkomm!* It's so *gut* to see you." Julia rushed over to hug each woman. How fitting that Martin's mother was her first official customer. But Julia would never tell the woman that her son had just left.

"And it's *gut* to see you, as well." Linda smiled.

"*Ja*, we have missed you," Lori said.

Out of the windows, Julia saw little Rachel, Sarah

and Abby stepping up onto the porch. They came inside, their cheeks and noses bright red from the cold.

"Oh, it's so *gut* to see all of you," Julia exclaimed. "I'll bet you would like one of these."

Leaning down at eye level, she held out the tray of cookies to little Rachel and smiled as the child chose a frosted snowman.

The doorbell tinkled again. Before Julia knew it, the store was filled with happy chatter and laughter as several ranchers' wives and people from town came inside to inspect her wares. Julia soon found herself embroiled in explaining the various scents and ingredients of her products. Between keeping the cookie tray and punch bowl filled, Mom also ran the cash register. As she tended to her customers, Julia lost track of the many sales they made.

"Do you have anything without scent?" Sarah Yoder asked.

Ah! Thankfully, Julia had thought about her Amish customers and their desire to live a simple life.

"*Ja*, I've got a lovely plain soap with no added fragrance or colors." Julia lifted a creamy-looking white bar to show the woman. "It lathers beautifully—"

A harsh gasp caused her to turn. Marva Geingerich stood just in front of the open door, clutching her gray woolen gloves in her hands. White snowflakes dotted her black traveling bonnet, melting into little droplets of water. She must have just arrived and was staring across the room at Sharon.

"I knew I recognized you." Marva's loud voice carried across the room.

Mom stood at the cash register, speaking to Essie Walkins, the owner of Tigger the cat. As Mom reached for a bar of lavender soap, she looked up and saw Marva. An expression of surprise drained Mom's face of color.

Marva lifted a bony finger and pointed at Sharon. "Now I remember where I know you from. Your *vadder* was Michael Miller and you abandoned your faith when you were eighteen years old to marry an *Englischer*. When you left, you broke your poor *mudder*'s heart. She died a year later, followed by your *vadder* only months after that. It's no wonder you ran away and were never heard from again."

A hush fell over the entire store. Everyone stopped and stared, their eyes filled with shock. Even the townsfolk, who had no idea what Marva was talking about, looked shocked and uncomfortable.

Sharon's spine stiffened and she lifted her chin higher. "I don't know what you're talking about. I am not Amish."

Without another word, Mom turned and walked out of the room. Julia stared after her, her mind racing. Marva's words played over and over again in her brain. She didn't know what to think. She couldn't breathe. Couldn't move. A myriad of thoughts scrambled inside her mind. A sick feeling settled in the pit of her stomach. She didn't know what was going on but she intended to find out.

"Linda, would you mind tending to the store for a few minutes, please? I'll be right back," Julia said.

Linda nodded with understanding and Julia handed her the bar of soap she'd been holding. She hurried across the room and down the hallway.

She found Mom upstairs in their apartment, the door closed and locked firmly.

Julia rapped on the wooden panel. "Mama, it's me. Will you open the door, please?"

"No, not now. Go away!" came Sharon's reply.

Julia knocked again. "I'm worried about you. I'm not leaving, so you'd better open the door now."

A long pause and then she heard the lock click. Turning the knob, she stepped inside and found her mother sitting on the sofa, her face buried in her hands.

"Mom, what is going on?" Julia sat beside her mother and rested a hand on her back.

Mom sniffed and sat up straight, staring across the room. Her eyes were red with tears. "I… I hoped you would never find out."

"Find out what?"

"That…that I was raised Amish."

Julia gasped. "Oh, Mom. What are you saying?"

"It's true. I… I was raised Amish. I left the faith in order to marry your father over twenty-six years ago."

Julia's mind went blank. This was news to her. All her life, neither of her parents had given her a clue that her mother had been raised Amish. They'd told her that Mom's parents had died. Apparently, that was true but why hadn't they told her the full truth?

"I was treated very harshly by my family and church elders," Mom continued. "Oh, please, Julia. Please don't join their faith. I beg you. It isn't just a commitment of faith but would require a change to your entire way of life."

"I've already told you I'm not planning to join their church," Julia said.

"That's good. If you join them and marry Martin, their church elders won't let you visit me anymore because I was raised Amish and abandoned the faith. They'd shun me."

Julia covered her mouth with her hand to keep from crying out. "No, Mom. Tell me this isn't true."

Mom met her gaze and Julia saw the tears streaming down her cheeks. "I'm afraid it is. Now you know why I've fought so hard against you spending time with Martin. Neither my Amish family nor your Grandpa Walt approved of your father and I marrying. They all tried to break us apart. So we left Ohio and moved to Kansas, seeking a fresh start. In his anger, your father refused to speak to your Grandpa Walt again. We thought it best that I keep my past life a secret from everyone, including you."

"But why tell me now?" Julia cried.

"Because Marva Geingerich recognized me and I can't lie to you any longer. Marva never was a nice woman. Always so harsh and judgmental. That's how I was treated by everyone when I left to marry your father."

Julia cringed. She figured there were good and bad people in all faiths and nationalities. She shook her head, hardly able to believe what her mother had told her. Now, everything made sense. The secretiveness, the disapproval.

"I think your Grandpa Walt regretted the fight he had with your father," Mom said. "That's why he left you this store. It was his way of making amends for past hurts. But I don't want to see you go through the same pain I was forced to endure in order to marry the man I loved."

Julia nodded in understanding and shock. "It's not an issue anymore, so don't worry about it."

Regardless of what her mother had told her, she could

never marry Martin. She'd promised her father she'd look after her ailing mother. There was no way for her to join the Amish faith and still be a part of her mother's life. Not as long as her mother felt the way she did toward the Amish.

During the church meetings and other gatherings Julia had attended, she'd heard a few whisperings about shunning. The only reason the Amish had welcomed her was because she'd expressed a deep interest in their faith and they thought she'd be baptized. But Julia would never turn her back on her mother. Crying about it wouldn't change a thing.

"I understand." Julia stood and reached for a tissue before wiping her eyes and nose. She couldn't sit here in the doldrums. She had people downstairs and a store to run. It was their grand opening and she intended to make the best of the day. Their livelihood depended on it.

"Where are you going?" Mom asked as Julia crossed the room.

Julia turned, her hand on the doorknob. Looking at her mother's pale face, she shrugged. "Downstairs. I have a store to run. Life must go on. But I love you, Mom, no matter what. Nothing will tear us apart. I promise you that."

Mom didn't try to stop her as she closed the door quietly behind her. Standing alone on the landing, Julia felt her heart breaking all over again. Except this time, she didn't feel angry. She just felt numb and empty inside. No doubt Linda would tell Martin what had happened and that Marva had recognized Sharon. The news would soon spread among the entire *Gmay*. Since Sarah was in the store when it happened, Julia figured Bishop

Yoder would hear about it before lunchtime. There was no way around it.

Julia couldn't see Martin tomorrow. No, nor any other day after that. After what had happened with Dallin, maybe it was best if she never loved again. Her path was set. She could never convert to the Amish faith. She couldn't attend church with Martin again and they could never be together. It was that simple.

Chapter Thirteen

It had been three torturous weeks since Martin had seen Julia. Three weeks since the grand opening of her soap store. With just two days before Christmas, he felt like a caged animal. Pacing inside his father's barn, he sought to relieve some pent-up energy. It was early afternoon and the snow had fallen deep, covering everything in a blanket of white. Otherwise, he'd go outside for a long, brisk walk.

Now, even the contented lowing of the milk cows couldn't soothe his jangled nerves.

He loved her. He knew that now. He couldn't get her off his mind. He loved her but he couldn't have her. And the pain was almost more than he could bear.

He stared outside the open door. When he exhaled, he could see his breath on the air. The pristine glow of new-fallen snow seemed surreal and lovely. It was a good day to stay indoors. He had no reason to go into town.

As promised, he'd gone to Julia's home early the day after the grand opening of her store. His mother had told him of its success. She'd also told him that Marva Geingerich had recognized Sharon from when they both lived in Ohio.

She'd told him Sharon was raised Amish.

Suddenly, everything made sense. Sharon's protests when Julia had accompanied him to church. Her refusal to join them at any Amish events. Her look of disgust whenever she saw him.

Sharon didn't want an Amish life for her daughter. In order to abandon her family so she could marry an *Englischer*, Sharon must have hated her faith. And yet, it couldn't have been easy, turning her back on everything in her life to be with the man she loved. Martin didn't want that to happen to him and Julia.

He'd been beyond disappointed when Julia didn't greet him at the door that morning. Instead, Sharon had presented him with a letter. He'd never forget the chill that swept over his body as Sharon handed him the envelope, then closed the door in his face.

He'd sat inside his buggy and ripped open the letter to read the pages. The message was simple and to the point. Julia didn't want to convert to his Amish faith. She expressed her joy and gratitude for him teaching her so much about Jesus Christ but asked that he not see her anymore.

He'd crumpled the pages in his fist, filled with such frustration and grief that he could hardly stand the pain. All his life, he'd been taught four key precepts: be slow to anger, slow to take offense, quick to repent and quick to forgive. These principles had governed his entire life. But now, he longed to cast them aside. To yell and scream and cry.

He loved Julia and wanted to make her his wife. He couldn't stand to lose her, yet that's exactly what had happened. The news of what her mother had done didn't diminish that love. Nor did it mean he didn't miss Julia like crazy. After all, it wasn't her fault that her mother had abandoned her faith. But he was a strong man. A man who loved God. And now, he must honor Julia's wishes even if it wasn't what he wanted.

"*Sohn*, it's too cold out here in the barn."

He jerked around and found his parents standing in the doorway. It was his mother who spoke. She wore her warm, woolen shawl draped over her shoulders, a fretful expression on her face.

"Why don't you *komm* into the house where it's warm?" David asked.

Martin turned away. His parents were the last people he wanted to see right now. "I'd rather stay here."

"You're pining for Julia, aren't you?" David asked.

A rustling came from the hayloft overhead but Martin paid it little heed. His thoughts were in turmoil. All he could think about was Julia.

"*Ja*, I miss her very much," he said.

"That's understandable. You love her," Linda said.

He couldn't deny it but he didn't acknowledge what his parents already knew. Surely the love he felt for Julia and the pain of losing her showed on his face.

"Even so, you must not see her again." David's tone was soft and sympathetic.

Hearing these words spoken out loud caused a panic like he'd never felt before to rush over Martin. His throat felt tight, his ears clogged. It was as if he were under water and couldn't breathe. He was drowning and couldn't save himself.

"But if she has an earnest heart and truly wants to

know more about our faith, we have an obligation to teach her," Martin argued.

"That time has passed, *sohn*. She has told you she doesn't want to convert so you must let her go. The Lord has something better in mind for you," David said.

Like what? What could be better than Julia? Nothing!

Martin looked to his mother for support. Surely she understood what he was going through. Her eyes were filled with tears, her face creased with sorrow but she didn't say a word. From her past examples, he knew she would never go against her husband's word. Not on something as important as this. And not if it meant she would lose her eldest son.

"You fear I might leave my faith in order to marry Julia," he said.

It was a statement, not a question.

"*Ja*, we know how strong love is. It can pull you in the wrong direction. But you must fight it, *sohn*. You must remain solid in your faith. Nothing can be stronger than your relationship with *Gott*." David spoke passionately, with all the love and conviction of a good parent trying to save his eldest child.

Strands of hay fell from above, wafting through the air. A low murmur of timbers hinted of movement in the hayloft and Martin thought a barn cat must be up there, nesting in the warm straw.

"I promise if you will hold firm, all things will be made right again. The Lord will bless you," David said.

His mother nodded in agreement.

Martin slashed his hand through the air. "Spare me your promises. I love Julia. She is the choice of my heart. And now you're telling me I can't have her."

Martin was a grown man. He should be able to choose

whom he would wed. But he also knew he must not challenge his church elders or his parents. To do so could put him in the position of being shunned by his people. Something he would rather avoid at all costs. But in his heart, the thought of never seeing Julia again left him feeling sad and empty inside. He couldn't stand to live without her. He couldn't!

David stepped over to him and rested a hand on his shoulder. "*Sohn*, we know you care for her. We all do. But she is *Englisch* and has made it clear she won't be baptized into our faith. You must not see her again. Do you understand?"

It took a long time for Martin to respond. And even as he said the words, it didn't ease his burden. "*Ja*, I understand."

"*Ne! Ne!*"

The cry came from above. Hank appeared suddenly, poking his head over the edge of the hayloft. As they stared in shock, he scrambled down the ladder. He stood before them, strands of hay sticking to his hair, gloves and coat. He must have been up there listening all this time.

"Julia is my girl. She's not gonna marry Mar-tin. She's gonna marry me," the boy yelled as he jerked his thumb toward his chest.

"*Ach*, Hank. Julia isn't going to marry you. She isn't going to marry Martin either. Don't be *dumm*," David said, shaking his head with impatience.

"*Ja*, she is. You're trying to steal my girl," Hank insisted as he glared angrily at Martin.

Before Martin could respond, the boy turned and raced out of the barn. He plowed through the depths of snow, running toward the brightly lit house.

"Hank! *Komm* back," David called, but Hank kept going.

Linda stepped over to the door, her features crinkled with concern. From her expression, Martin could tell she didn't like this contention in her family.

"David! Martin! Go after him," she cried.

"He's just blowing off steam. He'll go to his room and think about it for a while. It's best to let him be alone for now. I'll speak to him later," David said.

But that wasn't the case. When they finally went inside, Hank was nowhere to be found. The other children hadn't seen him either. And when Martin looked outside, he saw a trail of footprints in the new-fallen snow leading up to the main road.

"Do you think he ran away? It's too cold to be outside for very long and night is coming on," Linda said, wringing her hands in worry.

Martin took a deep breath and blew it out in a quick exhale. He had a bad feeling about this. Hank had run off once before after a bad fight with one of his sisters. It had taken the entire *Gmay* to find him the next day down by the creek. But that had been during the warm summertime.

Mamm was right. The winter coat, boots, scarf, hat and gloves Hank was wearing were warm but not if he got wet and not if he was outside for any great length of time.

"David! Martin! Please go find him," Linda pleaded, looking worried.

Martin hesitated, thinking fast. His father was a good, pious man but he had never taken Hank's tantrums seriously. Frankly, the man didn't know quite how to deal with Hank's Down syndrome. David loved Hank dearly but he didn't understand the boy and thought he should buck up and cope. He didn't realize how much Hank adored Julia.

Hank wanted to be a normal kid like everyone else in the *Gmay*. He didn't understand that his Down syndrome made it impossible for him to wed one of their Amish girls and manage a farm and family on his own. Martin hated to be the one to explain it to Hank.

Martin reached for his warm leather gloves and jerked them on. He hadn't had time to remove his scarf, coat and boots, so he was ready to go.

"I'll hitch up the horse to the buggy," he said.

"Where are you going? Just wait a while and he'll *komm* home on his own," David demanded.

"*Ne*, I don't think so. Not this time. I've got to find him and bring him home." Jerking open the back door, Martin stepped outside and headed toward the barn without a backward glance.

He was standing in the horse stall prepping the animal for a winter ride when his father found him.

"*Ach*, perhaps you're right, *sohn*. I'll go with you," David said.

Martin nodded, putting aside his own grief for the time being. Though he longed to resolve his problem with Julia, he must think of his brother now. Hank was mourning the loss of Julia, too. Martin should have been more understanding of his brother's feelings. He should have realized Hank was hurting. No matter what, Martin had to find the boy. He just had to. Grief and anger could cause Hank to do something very foolish and dangerous.

Martin had already lost the love of his life. He couldn't lose his little brother, too.

Chapter Fourteen

For the third time that morning, Julia counted the stack of small cardboard boxes she used to fulfill her online mail orders. Sitting in the packaging room next to her office, she felt a draft of cold air and shivered. It was Christmas Eve and she had just opened the store. From where she sat, she could hear the bell if someone entered the store and go wait on them. But since it had snowed nonstop all night and the plows were just now clearing Main Street, she didn't expect much business today. Thankfully, the storm had finally ceased. The local farmers were pleased by the moisture. So was she. It would ensure Martin had plenty of water for his crops next summer.

She counted the boxes again, trying to take her mind off him. How she missed him. For three weeks, she'd longed to get up the nerve to go and see him. But what would she say? He was Amish and she was *Englisch*. They were as different as night and day. But she loved him. She knew that now without a single doubt in her mind. He wasn't like Dallin at all. The fact that Martin had stayed away told her that he respected her and her decisions. She loved him and she couldn't be with him. Not as long as her mother disapproved.

She shivered again. Maybe the woodstove needed more fuel.

Scooting back her chair, she stood and poked her head into the hallway leading to the apartment upstairs. The back door stood wide open, a frigid breeze rushing into the building along with a spray of morning sunlight. She had shoveled the walk earlier. Though the skies were clear, it was still freezing.

Brr! Julia walked to the door and leaned outside. "Mom? Are you out here?"

"I'm in the store." Mom's voice came from the front of the building and she soon appeared in the hallway. "Did you need me?"

Sharon held a stick of kindling and must have been feeding the stove in the store.

Shaking her head, Julia closed the back door securely and locked it. "No, I was just wondering where you were."

Hmm. Maybe Mom had opened the back door to retrieve some firewood and then not latched it tight. It had happened before. She thought of asking Martin to repair the latch, but no. He'd do it in a heartbeat but it would only cause her more anguish to bring him back.

Julia turned away, still hurting from what Mom had told her three weeks ago about being raised Amish. Since that time, they had only briefly discussed the topic. Their relationship had changed somehow. All her life, Mom had kept this giant secret from her and Julia felt betrayed. It would take some time to rebuild the trust between them. And in the meantime, Julia was aching for Martin.

"Do you still want to close the store early today?" Mom asked.

Julia nodded. "Yes, we'll close at noon. After that, I suspect most people will be home with their families celebrating Christmas Eve."

Funny how Mom deferred to her on business issues. Julia was tired from all their hard work and they'd sold a lot of their products to local customers. No doubt Mom was fatigued, too. As far as Julia was concerned, their grand opening had been a huge success. She would close early and share a quiet dinner with her mom and celebrate the birth of the Christ child. Whatever else, Sharon was her mother and Julia had to forgive her. No matter what, she could never turn her back on her mom.

"I thought I'd make lasagna for dinner tonight. It's kind of a festive dish. Does that sound all right?" Mom asked.

Julia barely heard her mother's words. She was still lost in her own thoughts but nodded vaguely as she walked into the office.

The bell over the store door tinkled gaily and she turned. Mom followed as she walked down the hall and entered the cheery store.

"Martin!" Julia exclaimed.

He stood in front of the door with his father and Bishop Yoder. The three men looked imposing, wearing their black felt hats, gloves and warm frock coats. Their boots dripped water onto the large rug she'd laid in front of the door for this exact purpose.

Removing his hat, the bishop stepped forward. "Julia, we are sorry to intrude."

Each of their faces seemed drawn with worry, their eyes filled with anxiousness. Something was wrong.

"What is it?" She walked to them, conscious of Mom standing in the hallway but able to see and hear their conversation.

"Have you seen Hank?" David asked.

She shook her head. "No, I haven't." She glanced at Mom, who also shook her head. "Why? What's going on?" Julia asked.

"He's run away. He's been missing since early last night," David said.

"Run away? But why?" she asked.

"He...he had an argument and ran way," was all David would reveal. "We were able to track his foot-prints in the snow up to the county road leading into town but then they disappeared. We are worried about him."

A lance of fear pierced her heart. She was worried, too. It was fiercely cold and snowy outside. "He's been missing since last night?"

"*Ja*, and we thought he might have *komm* here," David said.

Martin didn't speak but Julia saw from his expression that he was beyond worried. She longed to speak to him. To ask how he was. To tell him how sorry she was for hurting him. But now wasn't the time. Not with both of their parents and the bishop standing near.

"No, I'm sorry. He hasn't come here," she assured them.

"If you see or hear from him, will you contact us im-mediately?" the bishop asked.

"Of course. I can even shut down the store and come help you look for him," she said.

David held out a hand. "*Ne*, that isn't necessary. The

entire *Gmay* is out looking for him. Just let us know if you hear from him."

"We absolutely will." She folded her arms and watched as the three men turned and left her store.

Martin looked back at her from over his shoulder, his gaze meeting hers. In that one glance, she knew he was worried.

Through the window pane, she caught a glimpse of several other members of the *Gmay* walking down the street. No doubt they were out searching for Hank. Under the circumstances, she didn't feel like she could join them. She'd quickly learned how the Amish grapevine worked and they wouldn't feel comfortable being around her now that she'd said she wouldn't convert to their faith.

Instead, she busied herself with tidying the store while Mom went up to their apartment to prepare supper. Frequently, Julia paused in her work to step outside onto the front porch and search the abandoned street for some sign of Hank. But she didn't see a thing.

Right at noon, she was restocking the lip balms and creams when Mom came into the store carrying her warm coat and purse.

"Where are you going?" Julia asked.

"I need more mozzarella for the lasagna. I'm just going to dash down to the general store. They're closing at one o'clock today, so I'd better hurry. I won't be gone long."

Julia stood and set the box of lip balms aside. "Why don't I go get it for you, Mom? I don't want you to slip and fall. Or I can go with you and hold your arm. It'll give us a chance to look for Hank while we're out."

"No, no!" Sharon waved her off. "I want to go alone. And they've probably found the boy by now."

"I hope so but there's no way for us to know since they don't have a phone."

"I'll ask Berta when I get to the store. She'll have heard if they've found him." Berta Maupin was the owner of the only grocery store in town and knew all the local news.

"Are you sure you want to go alone?" Julia asked again.

"Yes, I've been cooped up in this house far too long and need a good, brisk walk by myself. The doctor said exercise would help relieve my pain. The plows have been out and I'm sure the shop owners have shoveled their sidewalks. The afternoon sun has melted off a lot of the ice, too. I'll be fine."

Hmm. Mom acted like she really didn't want Julia to go with her.

"Okay, just be careful."

With a nod, Mom slipped out the door and hurried down the porch steps. After watching her go, Julia locked up the store and went upstairs. Spreading a warm afghan over herself, she reclined on the sofa, trying to read a book. Her eyes drooped wearily and she felt herself relaxing. Sometime later, she awoke with a start. How long had she been asleep?

Glancing at the clock, she realized it had been almost two hours since Mom left.

Something had roused her. Some small noise but she couldn't be sure.

"Mom?" she called.

No response. Julia sat up and folded the afghan, setting it aside. The fire in the woodstove had burned low and she stoked it up with fresh kindling. But where was Mom? What was taking her so long? And had they found Hank yet?

She turned, intending to go downstairs, put on her coat and boots and go look for her mother. A scuffling sound came from overhead, followed by the moaning of timbers. This old drafty building. It seemed she would never get used to all its creaks and groans.

Reaching for the doorknob to go downstairs, she hesitated. Hank was missing. Was it possible that he'd sneaked inside and gone up to the attic? It was dangerous up there and he knew it. Martin had told him not to go there again. Surely he wouldn't have disobeyed. Or would he?

Turning, she retrieved a flashlight from a kitchen drawer, then walked down the hall to her bedroom. Kneeling on the floor of her closet, she pulled the attic door open and peered inside. A whoosh of frigid air rushed over her. She really must have more insulation spread across the rafters. But that chore would have to wait until spring.

Stepping onto the narrow stairway, she flashed the beam of light along the rickety steps. Thick shadows gathered around her. A narrow ribbon of light came from the vent set high in the outer wall. It was so dark and cold up here that she was tempted to go back. But a low whimper came from across the room and she shined light in that direction.

A bulky shape lay huddled near the far wall. It moved, then stood up.

"Hank!" A flood of relief washed over her. The boy was here. He was safe! "Oh, Hank! What are you doing up here?" she called.

"Julia," he cried.

She took another step, beckoning to him. "Come here. It's all right. Come to me."

Stepping on the strong beams, he followed Martin's instructions not to walk on the drywall. She took his hand as she pulled him into her arms for a tight hug.

"Oh, you're frozen clear through. Let's get you into the apartment where it's warm."

Taking his hand, she urged him to go first down the rickety stairs. In her exuberance, she moved too fast and the rotted stairs gave way beneath her feet. She screamed, feeling herself falling. Suddenly, she found herself caught by two strong arms. They lifted her safely to the landing.

"Martin!" she cried, gazing into his eyes.

He held her close against his chest. She was so grateful to see him that she clung to his neck, unable to hold back tears of relief.

Within moments, Martin had pulled her and Hank into the safety of her bedroom. As he secured the little doorway to the attic, she looked up and saw her mother, Bishop Yoder and David all crowded in the small room.

"What…what are you doing here?" she asked, beyond confused.

"There's plenty of time to explain. But first, let's get everyone warmed up. Come into the kitchen." Mom waved to them all and they followed her, crowding around the small table and sitting on the sofa.

Within minutes, Mom had poured each of them a cup of hot chocolate and set out a plate of frosted sugar cookies decorated like candy canes for them to enjoy. Hank gulped down the liquid and asked for more. As he gobbled down cookies, Julia noticed he tossed hateful glares at Martin. The boy was obviously hungry but still angry.

Finally, Martin shifted nervously beside Julia, his gaze constantly returning to her.

"Are you all right?" he whispered.

She nodded, so happy to see him that she didn't even pretend to hide the love that must be shining in her eyes. She couldn't hide it anymore. Nor did she want to.

"How long have you been in the attic?" the bishop asked Hank.

The boy looked down and brushed some crumbs off his lap, an expression of shame covering his face. "All night. And it's really cold up there."

"All night? But when did you arrive in town?" David asked.

"Just a while after I left you last night. When I reached the main road leading into town, someone stopped and picked me up. They gave me a ride to town in their car."

"*Ach*, you could have been kidnapped," David said.

Within a few moments, he explained to Julia and her mother what had happened the night before when Hank ran away. Julia was touched by the boy's loyalty but wasn't sure how to handle his infatuation with her.

"Who gave you a ride?" Martin asked.

Hank simply shrugged. "I don't know. They were a *familye* with little kids. They were nice to me." He picked up another cookie to munch on, looking completely unconcerned by what he'd done.

It was a relief to know that Hank wasn't outside in the cold for very long. They were all outraged yet happy with this news. Outraged because they had no idea who had given him a ride but happy he was all right.

"But what brought you back here to the soap store?

How did you know Hank was here?" Julia asked the three men.

Mom shifted nervously. "I think it's now my turn to explain a few things."

Julia nodded, listening quietly to her mother.

"When I read your letter to Martin several weeks ago, telling him not to come see you again, I realized how much you truly loved him," she said.

"You…you read my letter to Martin? But that was private," Julia exclaimed, hardly able to believe her mother had violated her privacy in such a manner.

Sharon nodded. "I'm sorry, dear, but I had to know what you said to him. Then, I watched you over the past few weeks and saw how utterly miserable you are without him."

Julia just blinked, not knowing what to say.

"You don't laugh anymore," Mom continued. "You rarely even smile. You haven't made any new soap in two weeks. It's like the life has gone right out of you."

Yes, that was exactly how Julia felt. Losing Martin had drained her of all joy.

"Martin has been acting the same way. He's not himself anymore," David said.

Sharon nodded in understanding. "So, when I went to the grocery store today, I asked Berta if she would deliver another message to Martin. She agreed and drove to his farm for me. She spoke to his mother and asked her to send him here as soon as possible."

"*Ja*, my *mamm* brought me a letter from your *mudder*, explaining you were in trouble and needed me and asking if I would *komm* immediately," Martin explained.

"My mom did that?" Julia asked.

He nodded.

"And you came?" Julia said.

Another nod. "As quickly as possible. Of course, we didn't know yet that Hank was here, hiding in the attic. But we hoped you had found him."

Julia gave a quivering laugh. "I guess that was an added bonus for your trip into town. Thankfully, he's safe."

Martin laughed, too, gazing at her with adoration.

Mom lifted her head and glanced at the bishop. "I'm sure you've already heard that I was raised Amish. I hope the good things that have happened today will impact your decision to let Julia be a part of my life after she's baptized."

Julia inhaled a subtle gasp. Everyone in the room stared at Sharon.

"What are you saying?" David asked.

"Just this…" Sharon looked at Martin. "I want you to marry my daughter. She has my approval and my blessing to become Amish. But I don't want to be baptized. I made my choices years ago when I married my husband. I will love him to my dying day. But I want you and Julia to be happy and I know she won't be unless she's with you."

A shallow laugh escaped Julia's throat as Martin took her hand in his. Out of her peripheral vision, she saw Hank's angry glare. The boy obviously didn't like Martin paying her any romantic attention.

"Julia's my *maedel*," Hank said.

The bishop stood and opened his mouth to speak but Sharon cut him off with a slight wave of her hand.

Looking at Hank, Sharon smiled sweetly and leaned forward to cup the boy's face with her palm. "My dear boy, Julia is going to be baptized into the Amish faith and will marry Martin. Because she'll be your new sister-in-law, it won't be possible for her to be your best girl anymore. Instead, Julia will be your new sister. Doesn't that sound nice?"

Hank hesitated, thinking this over. Then, his eyes widened with delight and he nodded. "Julia will be my sister?"

Mom nodded, still smiling. "Yes, she will be your sister forever but not your girlfriend. Not anymore. Is that okay?"

Hank looked down, his forehead crinkled. Then, he nodded and grinned wide.

"*Ja*, I think I'll like having another sister very well. She'll make me cookies and soap," he said.

They all laughed.

"*Gut*," Mom said. She then spoke in perfect Deitsch to Martin, expressing her love for Julia and pleading with him to look after her little girl.

"Ahem! There's just one problem," Julia said. "I won't be baptized. Not if it means I'll have to shun my mother. I need to be a part of her life and I need her to be a part of my life, too."

A long pause followed this declaration.

"I believe that, since Sharon was never baptized into the Amish faith, she will not be shunned," Bishop Yoder said. "I see no reason why Julia cannot be baptized and marry Martin. Nor do I see any reason why she cannot be a part of her *mudder*'s life."

A startled gasp escaped Julia's throat. "Really? But I thought you would shun my *mudder*."

Martin squeezed her hand and she felt the surprised happiness emanating from him, as well.

"*Ne*, she was never officially a member of the Amish faith so how can she be shunned?" the bishop said.

"Oh, Martin!" Julia turned into his arms and he hugged her tight.

Julia hugged her mother, too. She was speechless as tears freely washed her face. "Oh, Mom, *danke. Danke*, my dear *mudder*."

They stood motionless for several moments, overcome by emotion. Then...

Martin leaned close and whispered something in his father's ear. David nodded, then cleared his throat.

"Ahem! I think we should leave these two young people alone for a while, so they can decide what they want to do." He lifted an arm, directing Hank to leave the apartment with him.

Taking his cup of hot chocolate, Hank went along willingly. Mom and the bishop followed, leaving Julia and Martin completely alone.

Tears flooded Julia's eyes as she looked up at the man she loved. "I don't know what to say."

He nodded, his eyes crinkled with compassion. "I do. I love you, Julia Rose. I love you more than anything. Please, will you marry me and make me the happiest man alive?"

"Oh, Martin! Of course I will. I love you so much. I was sick with grief when I thought I'd never see you again. I can't tell you how happy I am right at this moment."

Lowering his head, he kissed her. She clung to the folds of his coat, so happy that she could hardly contain the joy.

When he released her, he looked down at her, his eyes

sparkling with mischief. "I guess this means I won't be building a barn in the spring."

She tilted her head in curiosity. "Why not?"

"Because we're going to need to build us a house first. The barn will have to wait another year. I need to provide a home for my new bride to live in."

She laughed. "Do you think the bishop will coordinate another work frolic for us to build a house?"

He nodded. "*Ja*, I know he will. Once we're married, we'll need a place to live."

"We can stay here with my *mudder* until the work is completed on our own home," she suggested.

He frowned. "Do you think Sharon will mind? After all, you'll be Amish then and can't use electricity."

She pulled him close, snuggling against his solid chest. "*Ne*, she won't mind at all. She's given us her blessing."

He smiled and kissed her again. And after that, no more words were spoken. She had all that she needed and wanted right here in her arms. And her love and faith were the best Christmas gifts of all.

Epilogue

One year later

Julia stepped out onto the back porch of her new home and set the large wicker basket she was carrying onto the wooden bench. Like the spacious house itself, Martin had made the seat and most of the furniture inside with his own two hands.

A chilling breeze whipped past and she tightened her warm winter coat up high to her chin. Her sensible black tights and shoes weren't fashionable but they were warm and sturdy. She patted her white organdy prayer *kapp*, making sure her hair was pulled back into place.

The clothes of an Amish woman were quite plain but she loved her burgundy dress and its simple beauty. In fact, she found it comfortable and easier to move. As promised, Linda had kindly taught her to sew and Julia had made her dress and white apron herself. Though she was learning that *hochmut* was not of the Lord, she was secretly proud of her efforts. Between making soap, cooking meals and sewing clothes for her and Martin, she was learning something new every day. And loving every bit of it.

It wasn't easy juggling her work here at home with making and selling her soap products at Rose Soapworks, but she found that she enjoyed the challenge and would never begrudge her new life. The Lord had truly blessed her.

With some of the funds Grandpa Walt had left her, Julia had paid her new sales rep in Denver to schedule some ads on local TV. While Julia did the heavy lifting and soap making, Sharon did a lot of the desk work and was becoming quite computer savvy. She had reported that they'd received lots of raves from fans on social media. While Julia didn't own a TV or maintain her own website or social media accounts, she'd received several more wholesale contracts with some commercial vendors. Additionally, numerous online orders were constantly pouring in. Even with Mom's office help, Julia could barely keep up with the workload. And with the latest development in her life, she knew something would have to change in the coming months. And soon!

Taking a deep breath of cool, clear air, she gazed at the fallow fields glistening with a sheen of white. This past summer, Martin had fenced off a portion of his land and grown hay and oats. He hoped to save enough money to buy some Percheron mares and a stallion next summer. It had snowed two days earlier but the rainfall last night had cleared most of the white stuff off the county road. They should have no problem driving over to Martin's parents' house to celebrate Christmas dinner with them. Speaking of which…

"Martin! We're late! We've got to leave, my *liebchen*," she called toward the large shed in their backyard. Martin had built it to house their milk cow, horse and buggy until they could construct a giant barn in the spring.

At that moment, Martin came out of the shed, leading the horse. The animal was already harnessed to the buggy. Martin secured the shed door, then drove the buggy across the graveled driveway to park beside the house.

As he hopped out, Julia thought he looked more than handsome in his fine black frock coat and white shirt. Grasping her basket, Julia walked out to meet him. He took the basket from her hand and set it on the ground, then clasped her arm and pulled her close against his chest.

"*Guder mariye*, Mrs. Hostetler," he breathed against her lips before kissing her.

She swatted playfully at his shoulder and pretended to pull away. "*Guder mariye*, Martin. You know, someone might see us. It isn't seemly for you to kiss me out in the open like this."

She spoke entirely in Deitsch, having learned the language quite well over the past year.

He glanced around, as if looking for someone hiding nearby. "Who will see us on our own place? There's no one out here and we are most certainly alone."

To prove his point, he kissed her again and she didn't fight him at all. Not when she loved him so much. When he finally released her, she rested the palms of her hands against his chest and gazed lovingly into his eyes.

"Do you regret not being able to build your barn first?" she asked.

"*Ne*, of course not. We couldn't live with your *mudder* forever."

She arched her eyebrows in a playful glance. "Oh, I don't know. She didn't mind. Not really."

He snorted. "I don't think Sharon would like living with me the rest of her life. Besides, we will build the barn this next spring. I'll always choose you over worldly possessions. As long as I have you, I don't care about an old barn."

"But we won't always be alone, you know," she said.

He arched one of his eyebrows. "*Ach*, why not? Do you fear your *mudder* will need to come live with us soon?"

Lowering one hand, she rested it over her abdomen. "*Ne*, but our *boppli* will be here and you won't be able to take such liberties with me anymore. Nor will we ever be alone again."

He tilted his head to one side, his eyes crinkled in confusion. "Our *boppli*? Jules, are you…are you telling me that…?"

She nodded. "Uh-huh. We're going to have a new little one to join our *familye* soon."

Dawning flooded his eyes and a look of absolute joy covered his face. "A *boppli*? Truly?"

"*Ja*, we're going to have a *boppli* of our very own." She could hardly contain her own happiness as she shared this special news with him.

"Woo-hoo!" He picked her up and swung her around.

She laughed with abandonment, letting the dizzying joy fill her up. All her life, she'd longed for a home and family of her own. People to love and care for. And somehow, the Lord had blessed her with her heart's desire.

"You *bensel*. Now we are well and truly late for dinner at your *mudder*'s house," she teased him, trying to sound stern but unable to contain the laughter fizzing inside of her.

"*Ach*, so now I am a silly child, am I?" He opened the door to the buggy as she picked up her basket. He waggled his eyebrows and reached to lift a corner of the white cloth she had laid over top of the basket.

"What is inside?" he asked with a wicked smile.

Again, she gently swatted his hand. "Some pumpkin muffins, a fruit salad and an apple pie. Your *mudder* is preparing most of the meal, although I'm sure my *mamm* will bring something, too. Perhaps next year, we can hold the *familye* dinner here at our home."

He smiled with approval and held her arm as she lifted her foot onto the step and climbed inside. "You are becoming a very *gut* cook. At this rate, I'll become quite fat very soon."

He patted his lean abdomen for emphasis. Since he worked such long, hard hours, she doubted he would ever gain much weight but didn't say so.

"I'm afraid I'm the one who is about to gain some weight." Sitting in the buggy, she rested both her hands on her lower stomach and lovingly caressed the slight swelling there.

Glancing down, he flashed a wide smile. "I can't wait. The bishop has told me he will schedule another work frolic for us to have a barn raising in April or May. We'll have a new *boppli* to love and I'll get another field cleared and fenced off."

"*Ja*, it'll be a busy summer," she said. "We're getting so many orders at the soapworks that I'll need to hire some employees. I can ask the *Gmay*. I'll bet a couple of the girls or boys who are graduating from school might like a part-time job."

He tugged lightly on one of the ribbons on her prayer *kapp* before kissing the tip of her nose. "*Ja*, I'm sure they would. Is your *mamm* meeting us at my folks' house today?"

She nodded. "Now that she has bought a car, she is getting around the community quite well on her own. Lately, my mother is so happy that I can hardly tell she is ill. In fact, I think she's getting better every day."

Once she gave her blessing for Julia and Martin to wed, Sharon no longer took issue with the Amish people. Though she still missed her husband and adamantly did not wish to convert to the Amish faith, she attended many of their frolics and joined them for every family dinner.

"I can't believe the difference in her. It's like *nacht* and day," Martin said.

"I know what you mean. I think it's because she's so happy," Julia replied.

"*Ja*, contentment can change who we are inside. It can make us a totally different person," he said.

He closed the door and Julia sat quietly as she waited for him to hurry around the buggy and climb into the driver's seat. Though she was bursting with energy today, she also felt calm and tranquil inside. It was an amazing contradiction but she felt joyful and completely at peace.

Martin took the leather lead lines into his hand but paused, looking at her with a soft expression creasing his expressive eyes. "Tell me, when is our *boppli* due to arrive?"

Our baby! Oh, how Julia loved the sound of that.

"I'll need to visit the doctor in town, but I believe it will be the end of July," she said, unable to contain a smile.

He nodded, his eyes gleaming with delight. "In the

summer. Just in time for all the other new beginnings here on our farm."

Our farm! Again, Julia felt a flood of happiness flowing through her veins. This was her home. Their home! They had the soap studio in town, as well, but her mom was living there. Their farm was only two miles away and Julia went to work in town during the weekdays, to make soap and other merchandise and to package and ship her products all over the nation. But this farm and Martin were her home now. Forevermore.

"*Ja*, it seems like we're celebrating many firsts," she said.

He slapped the leads lightly against the horse's back. The buggy lurched forward. "Won't our *eldre* be pleased when we announce that we're expecting our first child this summer? Our *midder* will be so happy. It'll be their first grandchild."

"*Ja*, I know it will mean a great deal to my *mamm*," she said. "You know, one day she may be too ill to live at Rose Soapworks by herself. She is doing well right now but that could change."

Martin pulled the buggy onto the main road and the horse settled into a steady trot. Though it was cold outside, the sky was a clear azure blue with not a single cloud to mar this lovely Christmas Day.

"And when that time comes, she will move here to the farm so we can look after her," he said. "We will deal with it together, one day at a time. But I promise she will be cared for and you will always have Rose Soapworks for as long as you like."

Pleased by his words, she scooted over and hugged his arm. "*Danke*, Martin. You are so *gut* to me. I couldn't ask for a better Christmas gift."

He lowered his head and kissed her forehead ever so gently. "Nor could I. You have gifted me with so many treasures. The Lord has blessed us with so much abundance. This truly is the best Christmas ever."

As they sped along toward his parents' home, Julia could think of no better words to speak. She had her heart's desire. A large *familye* and friends to love and a husband who doted upon her. She breathed a happy sigh and enjoyed the ride. Her heart was so full and she couldn't ask for more.

* * * * *

If you enjoyed this
Colorado Amish Courtships novel,
be sure to pick up these previous titles in
Leigh Bale's miniseries:

Runaway Amish Bride
His Amish Choice

And don't miss the next
Colorado Amish Courtships novel,
coming in early 2020 from Love Inspired!

Dear Reader,

Have you ever wanted something so badly and it seemed you could never have it no matter what you did? In this book, Julia Rose has dreamed of having a large family all her own. She's been alone and willingly carried the burden of caring for both her ill parents for so long. Yet, when it appears she has finally found Martin, the man of her heart, she can't have him because he's Amish. Julia believes she is faced with the choice of abandoning her mother or turning her back on her love. Only when the people in her life make concessions that will allow Julia and Martin to be together does she discover that life is full of surprises and God can bless us when we least expect it.

I know that as we accept and wait upon God's will in our own lives and follow the Savior's example, we can find peace and joy no matter what difficulties we might face.

I hope you enjoy reading this story and I invite you to visit my website at LeighBale.com to learn more about my books.

May you find peace in the Lord's words!
Leigh Bale

COMING NEXT MONTH FROM
Love Inspired®

Available November 19, 2019

AN AMISH CHRISTMAS PROMISE
Green Mountain Blessings • by Jo Ann Brown

Carolyn Wiebe will do anything to protect her late sister's children from their abusive father—even give up her Amish roots and pretend to be Mennonite. But when she starts falling for Amish bachelor Michael Miller, can they conquer their pasts—and her secrets—by Christmas to build a forever family?

COURTING THE AMISH NANNY
Amish of Serenity Ridge • by Carrie Lighte

Embarrassed by an unrequited crush, Sadie Dienner travels to Maine to take a nanny position for the holidays. But despite her vow to put romance out of her mind, the adorable little twins and their handsome Amish father, Levi Swarey, soon have her wishing for love.

THE RANCHER'S HOLIDAY HOPE
Mercy Ranch • by Brenda Minton

Home to help with his sister's wedding, Max St. James doesn't plan to stay past the holidays. With wedding planner Sierra Lawson pulling at his heartstrings, though, he can't help but wonder if the small town he grew up in is right where he belongs.

THE SECRET CHRISTMAS CHILD
Rescue Haven • by Lee Tobin McClain

Back home at Christmastime with a dark secret, single mom Gabby Hanks needs a job—and working at her high school sweetheart's program for at-risk kids is the only option. Can she and Reese Markowski overcome their past...and find a second chance at a future together?

HER COWBOY TILL CHRISTMAS
Wyoming Sweethearts • by Jill Kemerer

The last people Mason Fanning expects to find on his doorstep are his ex-girlfriend Brittany Green and the identical twin he never knew he had. Could this unexpected Christmas reunion bring the widower and his little boy the family they've been longing for?

STRANDED FOR THE HOLIDAYS
by Lisa Carter

All cowboy Jonas Stone's little boy wants for Christmas is a mother. So when runaway bride AnnaBeth Cummings is stranded in town by a blizzard, the local matchmakers are sure she'd make the perfect wife and mother. But can they convince the city girl to fall for the country boy?

LOOK FOR THESE AND OTHER LOVE INSPIRED BOOKS WHEREVER BOOKS ARE SOLD, INCLUDING MOST BOOKSTORES, SUPERMARKETS, DISCOUNT STORES AND DRUGSTORES.

LICNM1119

Get 4 FREE REWARDS!

We'll send you 2 FREE Books plus 2 FREE Mystery Gifts.

Love Inspired® books feature contemporary inspirational romances with Christian characters facing the challenges of life and love.

FREE
Value Over
$20

YES! Please send me 2 FREE Love Inspired® Romance novels and my 2 FREE mystery gifts (gifts are worth about $10 retail). After receiving them, if I don't wish to receive any more books, I can return the shipping statement marked "cancel." If I don't cancel, I will receive 6 brand-new novels every month and be billed just $5.24 for the regular-print edition or $5.99 each for the larger-print edition in the U.S., or $5.74 each for the regular-print edition or $6.24 each for the larger-print edition in Canada. That's a savings of at least 13% off the cover price. It's quite a bargain! Shipping and handling is just 50¢ per book in the U.S. and $1.25 per book in Canada.* I understand that accepting the 2 free books and gifts places me under no obligation to buy anything. I can always return a shipment and cancel at any time. The free books and gifts are mine to keep no matter what I decide.

Choose one: ☐ **Love Inspired® Romance Regular-Print** (105/305 IDN GNWC)   ☐ **Love Inspired® Romance Larger-Print** (122/322 IDN GNWC)

Name (please print)

Address   Apt. #

City   State/Province   Zip/Postal Code

Mail to the **Reader Service:**
IN U.S.A.: P.O. Box 1341, Buffalo, NY 14240-8531
IN CANADA: P.O. Box 603, Fort Erie, Ontario L2A 5X3

Want to try 2 free books from another series? Call 1-800-873-8635 or visit www.ReaderService.com.

---

*Terms and prices subject to change without notice. Prices do not include sales taxes, which will be charged (if applicable) based on your state or country of residence. Canadian residents will be charged applicable taxes. Offer not valid in Quebec. This offer is limited to one order per household. Books received may not be as shown. Not valid for current subscribers to Love Inspired Romance books. All orders subject to approval. Credit or debit balances in a customer's account(s) may be offset by any other outstanding balance owed by or to the customer. Please allow 4 to 6 weeks for delivery. Offer available while quantities last.

Your Privacy—The Reader Service is committed to protecting your privacy. Our Privacy Policy is available online at www.ReaderService.com or upon request from the Reader Service. We make a portion of our mailing list available to reputable third parties that offer products we believe may interest you. If you prefer that we not exchange your name with third parties, or if you wish to clarify or modify your communication preferences, please visit us at www.ReaderService.com/consumerschoice or write to us at Reader Service Preference Service, P.O. Box 9062, Buffalo, NY 14240-9062. Include your complete name and address.

LI20

"Are the *kinder* okay?"

"Yes, they'll be fine." Uncomfortable with his small intrusion into her family, she said, "Kevin had a bad dream and woke us up."

"Because of the rain?"

She wanted to say that was silly but, glad she could be honest with Michael, she said, "It's possible."

"Rebuilding a structure is easy. Rebuilding one's sense of security isn't."

"That sounds like the voice of experience."

"My parents died when I was young, and both my twin brother and I had to learn not to expect something horrible was going to happen without warning."

"I'm sorry. I should have asked more about you and the other volunteers. I've been wrapped up in my own tragedy."

"At times like this, nobody expects you to be thinking of anything but getting a roof over your *kinder*'s heads."

He didn't reach out to touch her, but she was aware of every inch of him so close to her. His quiet strength had awed her from the beginning. As she'd come to know him better, his fundamental decency had impressed her more. He was a man she believed she could trust.

She shoved that thought aside. Trusting any man would be the worst thing she could do after seeing what Mamm had endured during her marriage and then struggling to help her sister escape her abusive husband.

"I'm glad you understand why I must focus on rebuilding a life for the children." The simple statement left no room for misinterpretation. "The flood will always be a part of us, but I want to help them learn how to live with their memories."

"I can't imagine what it was like."

"I can't forget what it was like."

Normally she would have been bothered by someone having sympathy for her, but if pitying her kept Michael from looking at her with his brown puppy-dog eyes that urged her to trust him, she'd accept it. She couldn't trust any man, because she wouldn't let the children spend their lives witnessing what she had.

Don't miss
An Amish Christmas Promise *by Jo Ann Brown,*
available December 2019 wherever
Love Inspired® books and ebooks are sold.

LoveInspired.com